LOVE AND KISSES

Jean Ure

HarperCollins *Children's Books*

For Zoe Crook

First published in Great Britain by HarperCollins *Children's Books* in 2009
HarperCollins *Children's Books* is a division of HarperCollins*Publishers* Ltd,
77-85 Fulham Palace Road, Hammersmith, London W6 8JB

The HarperCollins *Children's Books* website address is
www.harpercollins.co.uk

1

Text © Jean Ure 2009
Illustrations © HarperCollins*Publishers* 2009

The author and illustrator assert the moral right to be
identified as the author and illustrator of this work.

ISBN-13: 978-0-00-728172-5

Printed and bound in England by
Clays Ltd, St Ives plc

CHAPTER ONE

I'll never forget the day I first saw Alex. I was walking down Hawthorn Road with my best friend Katie. Best friend in the whole world! Friends for ever, through thick and thin. Though that was the summer we *almost* parted company... and all because of Alex.

It was a Friday, I remember; the second half of the

summer term. Katie was coming back to my place for a sleepover, which was something we quite often did. Either her place or mine; we used to take it in turns. That day it was my turn, so there we were, happily wandering down the road together in the sunshine, carting our school bags full of the usual massive amounts of homework, when WHAM! Bam! It hit me.

A few doors away from my place, they were turning one of the big houses into flats. The other morning I'd seen an older man, who seemed to be in charge; but he wasn't there that Friday. Or maybe he was, but he was indoors. Outside, in the front garden, there was a red-haired boy churning stuff about in a cement mixer. As we walked past, he turned to look in our direction and winked. He did! He *winked*. I tried to pretend I hadn't noticed, but it still made me get all red and flustered. Pathetic, I know, but you can't always control these things. It's an instinctive reaction. Very embarrassing.

I strode on, really fast, with my cheeks sizzling. A second boy was coming round the side of the house with a wheelbarrow. I caught his eye, *absolutely without meaning to*, and he smiled. Straight at me. At *me*! At *me*! OMIGOD. That was it. That was when it happened. The wham and the bam, and my heart going into convulsions. I felt like I'd been struck by lightning.

Katie came scurrying after me. "Really," she grumbled, "that was *so* not politically correct."

I mumbled, "What?" My cheeks were still sizzling.

Katie said, "What d'you mean, *what*?"

"What was not politically correct?"

"What he did! *Winking*. He winked at us! Don't tell me you didn't see?"

I muttered that I had tried not to take any notice.

"Oh, well, yes, me too," agreed Katie.

"Otherwise they think you're encouraging them." And then she giggled and said, "What about the other one?" She nudged at me with her elbow. "Know who he looks like?"

I shook my head. I tried to say "Who?" but I couldn't seem to get any sound out.

"He looks *exactly* like Jimmy Doohan."

It was true! No wonder my heart was walloping. Jimmy Doohan is this boy at our school. He's Year 12, now. He was Year 11 then, and half the school were crazy about him, including me and Katie. Not that he would ever have looked twice at us, even apart from the fact that we were only Year 8s. Me and Katie aren't the sort of girls that boys ever look twice at. Not that we're specially unattractive, or anything; just that we tend to stay in the background. I guess if you want to be taken notice of, you have to make a bit of an effort. Unless, of course, you are so stunningly drop-dead gorgeous that all eyes just automatically turn in your direction…

Jimmy Doohan was drop-dead gorgeous. Thick black hair, and coal-dark eyes and a face that was square and sort of… *chiselled.*

Katie was right. The boy who had smiled – at me, at me! He'd smiled at *me* – could almost have been Jimmy's brother. (I used to think of him as Jimmy, although I'd never said so much as a single word to him so he probably wasn't even aware of my humble existence.)

"See what I mean?" said Katie, turning to look back.

I couldn't resist a bit of a look back myself. The boy had emptied his wheelbarrow and was trundling it away, towards the side of the house. When he saw us looking, he raised a hand and smiled again. O! My! God! I nearly died. My cheeks were like a blast furnace.

Katie tossed her head and said, "*Well.*" I was too busy being incinerated to say anything at all. If my cheeks had got any hotter I might have actually burst into flames. You read about people doing that. One minute they're there, the next they're a pile of ashes. Something to do with their electrical systems shorting out. Which was what I felt mine were about to do.

"How about *that*?" said Katie. She sounded almost triumphant. I looked at her, rather anxiously. I did hope she wasn't deluding herself, thinking she was the one he had smiled at. Cos she wasn't, it was me! I was the one he'd seen first. Maybe if she'd been the one... thing is, I'm trying to be fair. I'm not saying I'm any better-looking than she is.

We both have our strong points – and our weak ones.

On the plus side, I am quite tall and reasonably slim and have nice eyes (or so I have been told). I also have long blondish hair, which I have a nervous habit of hooking over my ears when I am embarrassed or can't think of anything to say. On the minus side – well, I have to admit that I am not very pretty. My face is rather long, as is my nose. But I am not ugly!

Neither is Katie. She is probably a bit prettier than I am actually, with this little round face and rosebuddy mouth. Her hair is a sort of brown colour and curly, and cut quite short. Those are her pluses. Her really *big* minus is her bum. She says herself it is like two pumpkins in a bag, and that her legs are like tree trunks. On the other hand, she looks kind of cute in our rather yucky school uniform and I do envy her nose. I would swap my nose for hers any day!

Katie chattered excitedly all the way up the road. "I bet he's foreign! He looks foreign. Maybe he's Irish. Jimmy Doohan's Irish. Lots of Irish guys come over here and work on the buildings. Jimmy Doohan's dad is a builder. Did you know that? Jimmy Doohan - "

Oh, dear! She really did believe he had smiled at her. At least it gave me the chance to cool down and stop myself combusting. But in the end I had to say something, cos I just couldn't bear it any longer.

"Why d'you suppose it's OK to smile but not to wink?"

"Interesting," said Katie.

"I mean, it is," I said, "isn't it?"

"Yeah… I guess."

"So what's the difference?"

"Winking is rude," said Katie. "Smiling is… "

"What?"

"Smiling is friendly!"

I was so glad that the Jimmy Doohan boy had smiled and not winked.

We got home to find Ellie arguing with Mum in the kitchen. Ellie is my little sister – well, half-sister, to be accurate. She has a tendency to argue. She is one of those people who can't take no for an answer. In this case, *no* to going up to London with her boyfriend.

Boyfriend, for heaven's sake! She was only ten years old. If I'd have been Mum I would have asked her, "What are you talking about, *boyfriend*?" But that wasn't what was bothering Mum. She just didn't like the idea of them going up to London on their own.

"What would you do there?"

Ellie, virtuously, said they wouldn't do anything.

"So what would be the point of going? If you weren't going to do anything?"

Ellie said, "We just want to *be* there. Just look around."

"Like you haven't already been there about a thousand times!"

"That's different," said Ellie. "That's with you and Dad. I want to go with Obi."

What kind of a name is Obi?

"*Pleeeeze*, Mum… *pleeeeeze* let me!" She did this thing that she does, this girly thing, clasping her hands to her chest and making her eyes go all big. "We'll just jump on the tube and sit there good as gold till we get to Leicester Square."

"Then what?" said Mum. I could tell that she was weakening; so could Ellie. Mum is *so* predictable. And Ellie knows just how to play her. Brightly she said, "Then we'll get out! Then we'll *walk* up Charing Cross Road and we'll *walk* along Shaftesbury Avenue and we'll *watch out* for the traffic and we *won't speak to anybody* and then we'll *gaze* at all the theatres and I'll-imagine-how-it-will-be-when-my-name-is-up-in-lights!"

She gabbled this last bit in a kind of ecstasy. It made Mum laugh, just as Ellie had known it would. Mum is such a soft touch where Ellie is concerned.

"Have you asked Obi's mum about this?" she said.

Ellie smiled one of her cute little girly smiles. People just can't resist her when she does that. "I thought I'd try asking you first."

"Because Obi's mum would say *no*. I'll tell you what I'm prepared to do... I'm not having you roam around London by yourselves, but – *but* – " Mum held up a hand as Ellie opened her mouth to protest – "I'll take you both to a matinée of *Guys And Dolls*, if you like.

That was the one you wanted to see, wasn't it?"

Ellie gave a loud shriek. "*Mum!* Can you get tickets?"

"I think I could wangle it," said Mum. "Then we could go backstage afterwards. How about that?"

"Oh, Mum, *thank* you! Thank you, thank you!" Now we had the kissy huggy bit, with Ellie launching herself at Mum across the kitchen and nearly throttling her. "Dearest, darlingest, sweetest, *bestest* Mum of all time!"

Yuck, yuck, triple yuck.

"You'd better go and check with Obi's mum and see if it's OK with her."

"It will be, it will be!"

"Well, go and make sure. Katie, Tamsin! Are you OK, girls? I didn't mean to ignore you."

But with Ellie around she generally does. It's not her fault; Ellie has one of those personalities that just swamps everything. I guess she can't help it, any more than I can help being… well! A bit *inward-looking*, I suppose you would say. Like on one of those scales of introversion and extroversion, me and Ellie would be at totally opposite ends.

"Are you going to eat tea down here with us?" said Mum. "Or do you want to take it up to your room?"

I said we'd take it up to my room.

"So they can have *secrets*," said Ellie.

"That's all right," said Mum. "It's allowed."

"Don't know what they've got to have secrets *about*."

I said, "No, because it's secret. Moron!"

Ellie stuck her tongue out. Really quite pathetic. One minute she's trying to be just *so* sophisticated, wanting to go up to town with her *boyfriend*. The next she's behaving like a five-year-old.

"C'mon!" I snatched up a packet of biscuits and a couple of cartons of juice and headed for the door. "We'll be down later. What time's Dad getting back?"

Mum said, "Your guess is as good as mine. You know what these things are like."

I explained to Katie as we went upstairs that Dad was appearing in a beer commercial.

"Sometimes they just go on shooting for ever. When he did the drink-drive thing it went on till nearly midnight."

"That's mad," said Katie. "When you think it all ends up as just a few seconds on the screen."

I said, "Yes, I know, the whole business is bonkers. But Dad doesn't mind cos he gets paid overtime."

Some of the kids at school are well impressed that my mum and dad are in show business. I was famous for weeks after the drink-drive ad. *That's the girl whose Dad's on the telly.* Come to think of it, maybe Jimmy Doohan might know who I am! Though I don't see him as being the sort of guy that's easily impressed. I'm not impressed cos I'm used to it; and Katie isn't, either, cos she's known me since Infants, so she's used to it too. She can remember a time when both Mum and Dad had been out of work – pardon me, I mean *resting* – for so long that I almost couldn't go to school because my one and only pair of shoes had sprung a leak. I had to stuff them with newspaper! *Not* very glamorous.

"I'm glad my dad doesn't have to work odd hours," said Katie, as we reached the safety of my room and could chat without fear of little sharp Ellie ears picking everything up. "I like that he comes home the same time every night. Ellie'd probably say that's really boring of me, but I don't care! Sometimes I like boring."

I said, "Mm. Me too." Unlike Ellie, I have no ambitions to go into show business.

"Do you think we *are* boring?" said Katie.

It was one of my secret fears. But I wasn't about to confess it. "We're just us," I said. "Like Ellie is just Ellie. And she's way too young to have a boyfriend! How can you have a boyfriend at her age?"

I didn't even have a boyfriend at my age. Nor did Katie. We'd been *out* with boys; we weren't totally sad. But there's a difference between occasionally going out and having an actual boyfriend. Ellie was so… there was a word. I couldn't think what it was. Precocious! That was it. Acting like she was far older than she really was.

Maybe me and Katie acted like we were far younger

than we really were? Thirteen years old and no boyfriends. Soon we would be fourteen. And still no boyfriends!

We were good girls, me and Katie. All the teachers liked us; and on the whole we liked them. We did all our homework, we passed all our exams. We actually *enjoyed* learning stuff. God, this was seriously weird! There had to be something wrong with us. Why couldn't we just do normal things the same as everybody else? Skipping homework, bunking off school, going to parties, getting drunk. *Having boyfriends.*

"Ten years old," said Katie. She shook her head. "What were we doing when we were ten years old?"

"Dunno," I said. "Can't remember."

"We weren't still playing with dolls, were we?" Katie sounded suddenly anxious. "Please say we weren't playing with dolls!"

"No! Of course we weren't. We were – "

"What? We were what?"

"Well, we weren't painting our nails green and

wearing black lippy," I said. "And we certainly weren't going up to town with boys!"

There was a pause; then we both sighed, in unison.

"We're starting to sound like my dad," Katie said.

Hang on a minute! Katie's dad is old. But I mean *really* old. Like he's even talking of retiring. We looked at each other, stricken.

"No, but I mean," said Katie, "really! London is a dangerous place for a ten-year-old."

"With or without a boyfriend." Who in any case wasn't any older than she was. You couldn't call a ten-year old a *boyfriend*. It was ridiculous! "Have a biccy," I said. I didn't want to think about it any more. My precocious little sister, always getting in ahead of me. Always doing things *first*. And being allowed to get away with it! It wasn't that I was jealous of Ellie; it really wasn't. But I guess sometimes I did envy her.

That night, squashed up in my not terribly big bed with Katie, I lay awake thinking of the boy who looked like Jimmy Doohan.

CHAPTER TWO

He wasn't there on Saturday morning when we wandered past the building site on our way to the shopping centre. He still wasn't there when we came back. He wasn't there later on, when we went for a walk. A walk! Dad was very bemused.

"*Walk?*" he said, as we stampeded past him in

our eagerness to get out. "You're going for a *walk*?"

Honestly! As if we'd lost the use of our legs. Just cos he goes everywhere by car.

"We need air!" yelped Katie.

"And exercise," I said, looking rather pointedly at Dad, who instantly pulled his stomach in. There is a reason he'd been chosen for the beer commercial!

"Yes, right, fine," said Dad. "A walk in the park… admirable!" He held open the front door, elaborately ushering us out. "Off you go!"

So off we went, though in totally the wrong direction for the park. *Up* the road, *past* the new flats, *round* the block, *all the way back* – still nothing! The older man was there, poking about at the brickwork; but not a sign of Jimmy Doohan. The red-haired boy appeared, carrying a bucket. We didn't care about him. We wanted Jimmy Doohan! Where had he gone???

We didn't admit to each other that we were looking for him. That would have been too gross!

"I wonder if they work on Sundays?" I said.

"Might go to church," said Katie. "You know, if he's Catholic… if he's Irish."

"But shops open on Sundays." People still worked in shops.

Katie said, "Mm… " And then, "We're visiting my nan tomorrow." Like that had anything to do with it. But I knew what she was thinking. I could come and walk past the building site all by myself!

Which I did. I told Mum I was going to the newsagent to buy a magazine. I might just as well not have bothered, cos even the older man wasn't there. This was starting to become a bit scary. Suppose the boys had just been helping out for that one day? I couldn't bear it! Already I was getting obsessed. I kept remembering the way he'd smiled. A little bit shy. A little bit… uncertain, like he wasn't quite sure it was the thing to do. Unlike the rude winking boy, who obviously thought *far* too much of himself. I didn't care if I never saw him again. But Jimmy… he was even better-looking than the real Jimmy. And he'd smiled at me. At *me*!

Why hadn't I smiled back? *Why hadn't I?* Because I was too stupid and turned in on myself. Unless maybe I'd smiled without knowing it? Like sometimes you do, automatically. I really hoped I had!

Monday morning, Dad drove me in to school, which meant we whizzed past the flats so fast they were practically just a blur. But Monday afternoon... He was there! He smiled at me again, and this time I *did* smile back. I suspect my face looked like the setting sun, but I did manage to smile.

And again on Tuesday. Morning *and* afternoon. And on Wednesday, and on Thursday. It was like he was keeping a watch out, making sure he was at the front of the house so he wouldn't miss me. Then on Friday I was late, cos of choir practice. I thought at first he wasn't there, and my heart just, like, *plummeted.* And then suddenly he appeared, racing down a ramp from a van on to the pavement with his wheelbarrow, zonk! Right into me. Well, actually I just managed to skip into the gutter, which was a pity in some ways cos otherwise he might have run me over and then help, help, I would have needed picking up and it could have been really slushy and romantic! Even as it was, it was *quite* romantic. First off, he dropped the wheelbarrow, looking absolutely stricken. Then I said, "Oops!" (which on reflection is a silly thing to say, but I didn't have time to choose my words) and he said, "Sorry! Very sorry! I hurt?"

Not Irish. Some kind of foreign.

I mumbled that I was fine, and he said again, "Very sorry! I not look where I go." I assured him that I was OK (unfortunately!) but he still seemed anxious.

"I really not hurt you?"

"No, honestly," I said.

"Is my fault! I very stupid person. I look, next time".

I said, "Me too!"

And then I idiotically stood there, not wanting to move but not able to think of anything else to say. Fortunately he was less tongue-tied than me, in spite of not speaking the language too well.

"You live in road?"

"Up there." I pointed.

He said, "Nice houses."

"They're just ordinary," I said. "I'd rather live in one like this."

He pulled a face. "This one old."

"I like old! I like to think of all the people who have lived there before."

"Ah! You – " He stopped and waved a hand, frustrated. "I not think of word!"

"It's history," I said. "I like history."

"History. Yes!" He nodded at the house. "Much history."

"Ours is new. It's quite boring."

"Not boring! Very nice."

We chatted on about houses for a bit; and then, just as I thought I should be heading home he said, "You like maybe go out with me some time?"

My heart immediately went into some kind of mad squirming overdrive. My cheeks lit up like beacons.

"I tell you my name! My name Alex. What your name?"

I swallowed. "T-Tamsin."

"Tamsin... OK, Tamsin! You like we go drink coffee?"

My head started nodding, up-down, up-down. It wouldn't stop!

"We go Sunday, maybe?"

Before I knew it, we'd arranged to meet up the road in Starbucks on Sunday afternoon. I went on my way feeling like I was drifting on a cloud. I had a date. A real date with a real boy! My first ever...

Me and Katie weren't doing a sleepover that weekend. We hadn't even officially arranged to meet, but I couldn't resist ringing her.

"Is it OK if I come round? I've got something to tell you!"

Katie said, "What? Tell me, tell me!"

"I can't on the phone. I'll come round!"

Needless to say, I looked for Alex as I went up the road. I was all ready to smile at him, and wave. I'd even got specially dressed up in my best pair of jeans and a new top. But he wasn't there. Only the older man and the other boy, who had the cheek to wink at me again in a decidedly *knowing* fashion, like "Ho ho, who's going out with my mate?" I ignored him. And I wasn't worried, now, about Alex not being there, because tomorrow I would be in Starbucks with him… yay! *Most* unlike me. I am not at all a showy-off kind of person; I leave all that sort of thing to Ellie. But yay again! I was going on a date!

Katie flung open the door the minute I arrived. She'd obviously been hovering there, eager to know what my news was. I must have sounded even more excited than I'd realised.

"OK!" She dragged me inside and hauled me up the stairs. "Talk!"

I said, "Right. Well! You'll never guess… " I hooked my hair back over my ears. "I'm going on a date with Jimmy Doohan!"

"*What?*"

"Jimmy Doohan." I giggled, in slightly hysterical fashion. "The boy from the flats on my road?"

Katie said, "You've gotta be joking!"

"I'm not joking. He asked me! Tomorrow afternoon…
I'm meeting him, we're going to Starbucks."

"You're going out with a boy from a *building* site?"

"Why not?" I bristled. "He's nice, he's polite. He's
foreign. Polish, I *think*. Maybe Russian? I don't know!
Anyway, his name's Alex and he's definitely not Irish."

Katie said, "Oh, well, that's all right then."

I had this feeling she was being sarcastic. I said,
"Jimmy Doohan's Irish. You'd go out with Jimmy
Doohan fast enough!"

"Jimmy Doohan doesn't work on a building site."

"He might do! In his holidays. How do you know?"

"Holidays are different," said Katie.

Of course, I suddenly realised: she was probably a bit
put out. Even, maybe, a bit jealous? Still, I didn't like the
thought of her feelings being hurt. She was my best
friend, after all.

"It's so weird," I said, "the way things turn out.
I mean, me living in the same road… if it had been you
living there, it'd probably have been you he asked."

"I wouldn't *go*," said Katie.

Well! How ungracious was that? And there I'd been, thinking we could chat about what I should wear, the way other girls do.

"No point getting the hump," said Katie.

Pardon me? I wasn't the one getting any hump!

"I just think it's a bit dodgy, going out with someone you haven't even properly met. I mean, who is he? You don't know the first thing about him!"

"So I'll find out," I said. "We'll talk."

"He could be *anything*."

"So could Jimmy Doohan," I said. "Who knows what he gets up to in his spare time? He could be a drug dealer, for all we know. Could go round bashing old ladies over the head. I reckon you have to have a bit of trust or you'd end up never going out with anyone."

She grew a bit hot and pink at that. I immediately wished I hadn't said it. But quite honestly you can't afford to leave these things too late or you'll run the danger of never getting going at all. Ellie might be only ten, but already she knew far more about boys than either me or Katie. The situation was growing desperate!

"Have you told your mum?" said Katie.

It was my turn to grow pink. She'd asked a good question, cos the answer was *no*: I hadn't told my mum.

"Are you going to?"

Slowly, I shook my head.

"Dunno why not," said Katie. "If there isn't anything wrong with him."

"There isn't anything wrong with him! He's really sweet. It's just … you know what mums are like."

"I know what mine's like; shouldn't have thought yours would mind."

Katie always says that my mum, being an actor, isn't as strict as other people's. Like she doesn't care what me and Ellie get up to. It's true she doesn't fuss and flap, but I wasn't sure she'd be too pleased at me going off on a date with a boy I'd only just met. She'd want to know who he was, and where he lived, and how old he was, and all stuff I couldn't tell her. All I really knew was his name, and that he worked down the road. It was probably guaranteed to get even my mum in a flap.

"So if you're not telling her... " said Katie.

"I thought I'd say I was coming round to you!"

There was a pause. "Is that all right?" I said.

For a moment I thought she was going to say an outright *no*, or even suggest she came with us. We were so used to doing everything together I could understand if she took it as her right. In the end, somewhat grudgingly, she said she would think about it. "I'll let you know."

I said, "Please Katie, pretty Katie, *please*!"

She didn't even smile; just repeated that she would let me know. I definitely sensed a coolness between us.

The last time we'd had a coolness was when Katie had been asked to Millie Simms's party and I hadn't. I'd felt really hurt. I'd almost felt that if I couldn't go then Katie oughtn't to, either. So I didn't hold it against her, but I didn't want to ask her to join us. She might be my best friend, but Alex had asked *me*. And I wanted it to be a proper date!

I wondered if perhaps I could tell Mum I was going round to Beth's. That's Bethany Dewar, who's in our class. She's not a particularly special friend, but she lives quite near and she knows about boys, and about the need for sometimes having to keep things from your mum. She's what my nan calls *fast*. Some of the girls say she's a slag, but that's unfair; she just has this reputation because boys find her attractive. What's so wrong with that? I wouldn't mind boys finding me attractive!

I decided that I would call Beth and tell her the whole story. In fact, to be honest, I was dying to tell her the whole story! Swear her to secrecy and soon it would be all over the place... *guess what? Tamsin Mitchell's got a boyfriend!* And at least that way I wouldn't run the risk of Katie having second thoughts.

I was sitting on the bus, on the point of dialling Beth's number, when a text came through. It was from Katie.

U can tell ur mum ur with me OK. I wont split. Luv Katie.

How do people exist without friends??? I wasted no time in texting back:

Fank U, fank U. I will do the same 4 U.

She rang me almost immediately to say that I wouldn't ever have to do the same for her "cos I wouldn't ever go out with someone I didn't want my mum to know about!"

"It's only just this once," I pleaded.

"That's what you say now," said Katie.

I couldn't help feeling a little tingling of excitement...

CHAPTER THREE

I spent practically the whole of Sunday morning trying to decide what to wear for my date with Alex.

First of all, I put on my best pair of jeans – skinny, with little diamantés – and a blue top. Then I thought maybe jeans might be a bit too boyish.

So I took off the jeans and put on a skirt, only the skirt

didn't go with the top, so I took off the top and put on a blouse, but the blouse had a weird flat sort of collar which made my neck stick out like a broom handle. (I have rather a *long* sort of neck, which Mum tries to make me feel better about by saying that it is elegant.)

Crossly I tore the blouse off and scrunched it up and shoved it in the back of a drawer. Why had I ever bought the stupid thing in the first place? Ellie wouldn't have done. She's hugely fashion conscious, is Ellie. Always *designer labels* and nothing older than about six months, cos if it's older than six months it's past its shelf life. And Mum encourages her! So does Dad; they both think looks are important. Which I guess they are, if you're going to be an actress. If you're just a boring boffin like me, then who cares? I'd always known I couldn't compete with Ellie, so I'd just never bothered. I always told myself that looks didn't matter. I might even have believed it… until now.

Suddenly, I was in a panic. I tried on another top, another skirt. A short skirt, a long skirt. A plain top, a stripy top. An off-the-shoulder top. A crop top. A dress. Another dress. Denim trousers, white; combat trousers, green. I even tried a pair of shorts! I was that desperate. In the end, with the entire contents of my wardrobe scattered across my bedroom floor, I went back to what I'd started with, the skinny jeans and the blue top.

At that point Ellie came battering at the door, demanding to be let in. She knows she has to knock, but it's a totally empty gesture since she never actually waits to be invited. She just barges her way in.

She said, "Yikes! What's all this?"

I said, "Clothes. What's it look like? Don't trample on them!"

"I can't help it, there's nowhere to walk. What are you doing? Are you going out?"

"What's it to you?"

"Just taking an interest. Where you going?"

"I'm going round to Katie's, if you must know. What d'you want?"

"Um…" She pressed a finger to her nose, then

giggled. "I can't remember! Why are you getting all dressed up just to go to Katie's?"

"Cos I want to. Get out!" I gave her a shove. "I'm busy!"

"Cool jeans," said Ellie. "Oh – " She stuck her head back round the door. "I just remembered… I'm on telly in half an hour!"

On telly! Pur-lease. One of about five thousand faces in a crowd. She'd gone to the filming of some kids' TV show. Now you'd think she was the big star.

"I'm sure they got me, I was smiling like crazy at the camera. Dad's going to record it!"

"In that case, I can see it later," I said. "Now, go! I've got things to do."

I wished I could have told her I had a date, but she'd never have been able to keep quiet about it. She'd go and blurt it out to Mum and Dad, and then they'd want to know who I was seeing and where we'd met, and I just knew if I said "He works on the buildings down the road" Mum would freak. Dad too probably.

I filled in the rest of the time until lunch by putting on

lipstick and taking it off again. Then putting it on again, then taking it off again. Then plaiting my hair, then unplaiting it. Then putting it up, then letting it down. God, this was frightening! I wasn't fit to go out on dates. I just had no sense of style whatsoever.

I went down to lunch minus the lipstick, with my hair hanging loose. Then immediately *after* lunch I rushed back upstairs and did my lips with Topaz Glow and put my hair into a sort of complicated pleat thing. That was better! Now I looked sophisticated. I felt it was important to look sophisticated. Alex wasn't just some silly little spotty schoolboy like everyone else went out with. He was practically grown-up!

"So when can we expect you back?" said Mum, as I left.

"Oh… I dunno!" How long should a first date last? Would we just have coffee and that would be that? Or would we… go for a walk, maybe?

"I mean, you're not planning to spend the whole evening round at Katie's? Because you know we're going to Giovanni's."

I said, "Are we?"

"To celebrate Ellie's first TV appearance."

She had to be joking!

Mum gave a little giggle. "I know it's daft, but the camera really loves her… they went back to her twice!"

Big deal. But what did I care? I had a date! I assured Mum that I would be back in plenty of time.

"You're sure you don't want me to take you over to Katie's? I can, if you like. And do you want one of us to pick you up?"

I said, "No!" And then, because it came out as a sort of yelp, I added, "It's OK, honestly. I can get the bus," and shot out of the gate and up the road as fast as my slinky strapless backless sandals would carry me. Which wasn't very fast as I kept falling out of them.

Alex was already there, in Starbucks, waiting for me. He was wearing jeans and a T-shirt, and looked just, like, totally gorgeous. There are some boys who can wear T-shirts and some who can't. I think it is so wimpy, for instance, when boys have these thin, white, weedy arms without any muscles, so that the sleeves just flap. Alex had arms that *filled* the sleeves. And they were heavenly brown, from all the healthy outdoors work that he did.

He stood up when he saw me. I thought that was just *so* polite. Most boys, at least the ones I know, just have no manners at all. Although maybe I'm being unfair; if you actually went on dates with them they might act a bit differently, and not treat you like you're just a piece of the furniture. Alex even pulled out a chair for me, which made me all flustered. I thought, God, why am I so pathetic??? Why couldn't I manage to be *elegant* for once, and show a bit of maturity? It's not much use, putting on lipstick and doing fancy things with your hair if you are then going to ruin it all by behaving like some kind of social retard.

At first, what with me being almost *completely* retarded – i.e. not saying a word – and Alex speaking so little English, it seemed like we were doomed to sit in awkward silence. I sought frantically for something to say, but my brain seemed to have gone into a state of permanent hibernation. If it hadn't been for Alex, we might never have said a word from start to finish. He ordered two cappuccinos, then smiled at me across the table and said, "I glad you here. I think maybe you not come."

I said, "W-why would you think that?"

"I not – " He waved a hand. "I not sure you like me. I not sure... you want see me. I hope – but!"

I said, "B-but?"

"If you not here ... " He smiled again, and my heart started on its walloping act. "I understand, but I be unhappy. I happy when I see you! I wait ten minutes... quarter hour. I think, she not come – "

"You've been waiting *quarter of an hour*?" My voice suddenly squeaked into action. "I wasn't late, was I?"

"You not late. I very stupid! I come early."

I said, "I could have come earlier, if you wanted."

"Then I be even more early!"

He grinned then, and I giggled. He was making such an effort in a foreign language I couldn't just leave him to struggle along on his own. By the time we'd drunk our first cup of coffee we were having almost a real proper conversation. I asked Alex where he came from and he said, "I come from Poland, from a leetle veellitch."

I didn't understand at first what he meant; I couldn't think what *a leetle veellitch* was. Alex said, "Leetle?" and held up a finger and thumb, about half a centimetre apart.

I said, "Oh! *Little*."

He nodded and said, "Yes! Leetle. A leetle veellitch."

I got it, then. "A little village."

We both laughed. Alex said, "My accent... not good. You teach!" So then we practised saying "A little village" until he had it right.

"You good teacher," said Alex. "You speak good. I understand! Sometime – not so good." He made quacking motions with his fingers. "Like duck! I not follow. You like person on radio!"

I told him that was because of Mum and Dad being actors and always going on at us to *speak clearly*.

"You going be actor?" said Alex.

"Me?" I said. "No way!"

"Why no way? You pretty! You be good actor."

I got all embarrassed when he said that. I wish I could accept compliments gracefully! I couldn't even shake my hair over my face to hide my stupid blushes. Quickly, I changed the subject. I said, "Tell me about you! Are your mum and dad over here? Why did you come? Don't you miss Poland?"

"I miss at first," said Alex. "My mum and dad, they stay. I call every day. I very... what the word?"

I said, "Homesick?"

"Homesick! I very homesick. Now not so bad. Specially *now* not so bad." He grinned as he said that, and I started blushing all over again!

So why did you leave?" I mumbled.

He hunched a shoulder. "No job. No money. My family... not rich. My dad, he not well. My mum, she work. Not earn much. No future. Not good. This – " he opened his arms – "this the place to be. Good job, earn money... pretty girl!"

He took my hand across the table. Hot tingles ran up my arm. A woman sitting nearby caught my eye and smiled at me. I smiled back.

"I want come last year," said Alex, "but my mum, she say wait. She say when you seventeen, then you go. How old you?"

"Me? I'm... fifteen. Nearly sixteen!" The words were out before I could stop them. I would have given anything to take them back, but I wasn't brave enough. It would make me look silly. But why did I say it? *Why?* Who would believe I was nearly sixteen? I did have my hair up, and I was wearing lipstick, and I know that I do look quite a bit older than my age, but... *nearly sixteen?*

I waited with heart hammering for Alex to laugh. Instead, quite seriously, he said, "So you still in school?"

I said, "Yes," and pulled a face, as if I'd rather not have been.

Then he did laugh. He said, "Me, I free... no more school! No more lesson! Out in the world."

"I wish I could be," I said. It was *absolutely* not true.

I like school! My tongue just seemed to be running away with me. Alex asked me if I'd like another coffee, but regretfully I said that I probably ought to be getting home. I could have rung Mum and pretended I was staying on at Katie's, but I already felt nervous about lying to her. Alex wanted to walk me back, so I said "just to the corner" in case Mum or Dad – or Ellie! Just as bad – happened to be looking out of the window.

It seemed for a moment, as we got to the corner, that he might be going to kiss me. I think I wanted him to. That is… I wanted him to want to! After all, it was what people did on dates. But in the end he changed his mind. Or maybe he hadn't ever been going to. Did that mean he didn't fancy me? *Oh, God, please don't let it mean that! Please!*

And then, very solemnly, he said, "You like see me again maybe?"

At which my heart gave this massive leap and I said, "Yessss!" and we immediately agreed that we would meet the following Saturday, same time, same place.

Alex said, "I look forward," and he squeezed my hand, very hard. And that was when I knew, without a shadow of a doubt, that I was about to fall in love…

I was aching to tell someone! Ellie was coming downstairs as I let myself in. She said, "Ooh, you're all *pink.*"

I nearly cried, "Yes, I'm in love!" But I managed to restrain myself. It would have been absolutely fatal to let Ellie know.

Even as it was she felt the need to go and tell Mum that "Tamsin's all pink… pink as a raspberry!" Which of course just made me go even pinker.

Mum laid a hand on my forehead and said, "I hope you're not sickening for something."

I gave a silly little giggle of excitement.

"You are just so weird," said Ellie. She turned to Mum. "We don't want her throwing up, or anything. D'you think she should stay at home this evening?"

I wouldn't actually have minded staying at home. If I'd stayed at home I could have wallowed in the bath, listening to music and dreaming. But Mum wouldn't hear of it.

"It's a celebration," she said. "We've all got to be there."

So we all trooped up the road to Giovanni's to eat pasta and drink champagne with Mum proudly explaining to anyone who would listen that "Ellie's just been on the television!" She did it jokingly, but I could tell that underneath she was simmering with a quiet, mumsy-type pride. I have to admit, when I saw the thing later, Ellie did look good. She was a natural! And I guess it was quite something to have the camera pick her out *twice*, in such a huge crowd of people. I didn't begrudge her her little moment of triumph. I might have done, once; but not any more. I didn't begrudge her anything any more. She could be on TV as much as she liked. I was going out with Alex!

I made a resolve that I wouldn't say anything to Katie even though I was bursting to let it all out. I could see that she didn't want me splurging all over her. I was quite surprised, at first break on Monday, when she dragged me off to a quiet corner and said, "Right! Tell! What happened?"

I said, "Nothing really *happened*. We just sat and talked, and then... he walked me home!"

"Did you ask him in?"

"No! Mum still thinks I was round with you. Can I be round with you again next Saturday? Cos I'm seeing him again then!"

Slowly, as if giving me up as a lost cause, Katie shook her head.

"*Pleeeze*," I said.

She sighed. "All right. If you must. What about our sleepover?"

"I could sleep over Friday."

"And then go off next day and meet *him*."

"Not until the afternoon."

"A secret assignation." She does choose good words. Of course, her mum is an English teacher. "So tell me what you've discovered about him."

It was all the excuse I needed. I said, "Well... he's only been here a little while, which is why he doesn't speak much English. *Yet.* But he will, cos he's really trying. He's Polish. He comes from a *leetle veellitch* – "

"You what?" said Katie.

"A leetle veellitch. It's the way he says it! It's so cute. A *leetle veellitch* … "

"Yeah, OK, I get it! Go on. What else?"

"The other boy – the one with red-hair – "

"The rude one."

"Yes. His name's Marek. They came over together. The older guy, the one they work for, he came from the same village. But he came two years ago. Now he has his own business."

"So how old is he? Your guy. Alex."

It gave me such a tingle when she called him that. *Your guy…*

"He's seventeen."

"Are you sure?"

"What d'you mean, am I sure?"

"You sure he's not older?"

"No! He's not older… his mum said he couldn't come over here till he was seventeen."

Katie said, "My mum'd do her nut if she found I was going out with someone that age."

I thought yes, well, Katie's mum was a bit of a mother hen. Katie is her only child and she must have been at least forty when she had her. Unlike my mum, who was still a student when she had me. And would also do her nut, in all probability.

"Doesn't he find you a bit young?"

I said, "No." I didn't confess that I'd lied about how old I was.

Katie said, "Maybe..." She stopped.

I said, "Maybe what?"

She nibbled on a fingernail. It's her thing that she does, like me hooking my hair behind my ears. "Maybe next time he should bring his friend with him and I could come, as well, and keep an eye on you!"

I was taken aback, to say the least. She didn't even *like* his friend; she thought he was rude. And why should she think I needed an eye kept on me?

She assured me that it was perfectly all right, she

wouldn't interfere. So why did she want to come? I didn't want her there! She might be my best friend, but just because you're best friends doesn't mean you have to do everything together.

"Thing is," I said, "Marek's already going out with someone." Liar, liar, pants on fire! "He's not really free to go out with anyone else."

"I don't want to go *out* with him," said Katie, nibbling and munching as hard as she could go. "I just thought I could come along to... watch over you."

"Honestly," I said, "I don't need watching over. Stop fussing!"

"I can't help it, I feel responsible for you." She looked at me, hurt. "Wouldn't you feel responsible for me, if I was going out behind my mum's back with someone who was seventeen? I hope you would, cos it's what friends are supposed to feel. And if they don't, then they're not being very good friends."

I didn't like the thought of Katie being upset. "Look," I said, "maybe later?"

"Later what?" she mumbled, ungraciously, as she munched on another nail.

"Maybe later you could come along." Except who would she bring? She didn't know anyone. A foursome might be fun, but she was right: three was definitely a crowd. In my imagination, Alex and I were already kissing and cuddling and holding hands... how would we be able to do that with Katie sitting there scowling all on her own? Maybe, after all, she and Marek could come along. He couldn't be too bad if he were a friend of Alex. I made a note to find out whether he really did have a girlfriend or whether I'd just made it up.

Katie took her finger out of her mouth and stuffed her hand under her armpit where she couldn't get at it. "I hope you don't think I want to *spy* on you," she said.

I said no, of course I didn't; though that was exactly what it felt like.

"I just think it would be... safer. I mean... seventeen! That's practically grown-up."

That was what was so exciting about it.

"He might want to do things." She whispered it at me, earnestly. "Things you don't want to do."

I said, "Then I wouldn't do them."

"You might not be able to help yourself! You might get carried away. People do," said Katie. "It's the way it happens. You don't *mean* it to. It's the heat of the moment."

Yes, and at that particular heat of the moment, thank God, the bell rang for the end of break. I was beginning to feel quite uncomfortable with this conversation. Loftily I informed Katie that she had a mind like one of those magazines you find in the dentist.

I told Katie that it was really nice of her to come, but honestly, I knew what I was doing!

CHAPTER FOUR

Who says dreams can't come true? On Saturday, when we met, Alex kissed me… French style, on the cheek. Really sophisticated! Maybe it's what Polish people do. But I bet Jimmy Doohan wouldn't! Or any of the boys in our class. Spotty things.

I know that's not fair. They're not all spotty and even

the ones that are can't help it. But they were just so *young*. I couldn't imagine going out with anyone so young!

After we'd drunk our coffee we went for a walk and Alex held my hand. Electric shocks went shooting up my arm and zinging round my body. His hand was warm, and a little bit rough from all the building work that he did. I didn't mind it being rough, I was just glad it was warm. I once had to hold hands with this boy called Roger Barlow in a drama class and it felt all damp and clammy. Horrid!

We walked along by the river, and I wished someone from school could see me. Preferably Beth, cos then the whole class would get to hear of it. Or maybe Kez Daniels. Kez is so pretty, and so popular, and she's been going out with the same boy for, like, just about ever. They are deep in love and hold hands wherever they go, even at school. Nobody laughs; it's too serious for that. I used to envy her. Sometimes, lying in bed at night, I even used to pretend to be her. Now I didn't need to pretend. I was deliriously happy being me!

I just wanted someone to see me… but nobody did. I don't know what I would have done if Ellie had appeared. My hand was glued so tight I'm sure I couldn't have pulled it away. Fortunately, walking along by the river is not Ellie's thing. I was safe for the moment…

"It nice, no?" Alex swung my hand as we walked. "Nice by the river… you like?"

I nodded, blissfully.

"Some girl, they no like walk. They say, no car, no go!"

I assured him that I wasn't one of them. "I love walking!"

"Me, I like too. But one day I have car. I save money, then I buy. Then we go all over! All over country. You like come with me?"

My heart almost burst. Alex dropped my hand and put his arm round me, instead. "I very safe driver. You be safe with me."

I felt safe. Completely safe. I think I would have gone anywhere with Alex.

Every day, now, both in the morning and again in the afternoon, he would be waiting for me at the building site and we'd stop and chat. Sometimes, if no one was about, he'd put his arm around me or hold my hand. Mum couldn't understand why I was so eager to be on time for school. Not that I have ever been one of those people who always sneaks in late, but now I was racing out of the door before I'd properly finished my toast.

"What's with all the mad enthusiasm? Have you got a secret admirer or something?"

Ha ha. Ellie sniggered; even Dad gave a little smile. Old boffin brain Tamsin with an admirer! *What a joke.*

One morning as I walked past the flats Alex wasn't there. Marek explained that he was working indoors. And then he winked and said, "Wait! I get." Putting both hands to his mouth he bellowed at an open window: "ALEXXXXX! YOUR GIRLFRIEND IS HERE!"

It did make me a tiny bit panicky, in case any of our neighbours might be about. The couple who live next door to us, Mr and Mrs Waugh (Dad calls them the Woffs) have always seemed a bit suspicious of our family, what with Mum and Dad being actors and Dad quite often being at home all day instead of out doing a proper job. Mum and Mrs Woff quite often have long gossipy chats together, so any news would be bound to get back.

"I see Tamsin's got herself a young man... works on the buildings."

I was living on a knife edge! I could be found out at any moment. But when Marek called me Alex's girlfriend, it made my stomach go all wonderfully hot and gooey. Just three short weeks ago I'd almost despaired of ever being anyone's girlfriend. Now here was this rude boy yelling it out for all the world to hear – and suddenly I didn't care if the Woffs *were* about. I didn't care if Mum did discover Alex and me were an item!

Marek gave me this big grin and said, "He come double quick! Break his neck, he not careful."

We both agreed that morning that we couldn't wait until Sunday to be together. Alex suggested we go to a movie. He said there was one on locally that I would like.

"We go Friday, maybe?"

Friday was good. I could tell Mum I was staying on for

choir practice then going round to Katie's. Just so long as I was home by eight-thirty, cos if it was any later they'd want to come and pick me up.

"I know eight-thirty is really early," I said, "but my gran's coming, and she's only here for one day, so I've got to spend a *bit* of time with her. She doesn't come that often and she'd be really upset if she didn't see me at all, so if we could, like, catch the early show?"

I gabbled the lies out so fast I'm not really sure how much of it Alex managed to grasp, but he didn't seem to think it was odd that I had to get home. He nodded when I said "my gran". We agreed to meet after school at the Pamino Bar in the high street, then go on afterwards to the cinema. I had to tell Katie, because of missing choir practice. She said, "Miss Morgan's going to be furious!"

"Just tell her I'm going to the dentist," I said.

"*Me?*" said Katie. "Why me?"

I said, "All right! I'll tell her."

"So where are you really going? Apart from meeting Alex."

It thrilled me every time she just said his name! I explained that we were meeting in the Pamino Bar then going on to a movie. Big mistake. She immediately wanted to come with us.

"You can't!" I said. "We can't both miss choir practice."

"Why not? If you can, I can!"

"I've got a good reason," I said.

"So've I, I want to see the movie! I don't see why I can't come with you. What difference would it make? I'd be quiet as a mouse! You wouldn't even know I was there."

When she saw she wasn't getting anywhere she said in that case why couldn't she just come along to the Pamino Bar and have a coffee?

She doesn't *drink* coffee.

"Why can't I do that? Just to say hello?"

How could I explain? When you're in love, every minute you're together is precious. You don't want other people there; you want to be on your own, just the two of you. Poor Katie, she had no idea! All the same, it upset me to think that she was feeling left out.

"You don't want me seeing him," she said, "do you?"

I told her that it wasn't that. "It's Alex," I said. "He's shy. Maybe when he speaks English a bit better... maybe then you could come along." In the end she accepted it, but I knew she thought I was being disloyal, going off without her again. For years we'd done everything together. I did so wish she could find a boyfriend of her own!

I asked Alex, when we met, whether Marek was seeing anyone. He said, "Yes, he go out with Polish girl. Marta. She over here one year already. She speak English very good! You like sometime we go all together some place?"

I told him that I would love to, thinking to myself that that was the end of any matchmaking plans I may have had for Katie. It was probably just as well. Unlike me, Katie would never get away with pretending to be fifteen. All the same, I was sad that we couldn't both have found boyfriends.

I have to admit that I cannot remember a single thing

about the movie we went to that day. I can't remember what it was about. I don't think I actually saw very much of it... anyone who has been in love will know. And anyone who hasn't - well, they will just have to use their imagination. I'm sure it is not too difficult! All I remember is the warm glow I felt inside all night.

I arrived back home to be greeted by the news that Dad had landed a part in a movie! Ellie, gloatingly, said it was a *real* part.

"A proper character, with a name. Tell her which character you're playing, Dad!"

Dad drew himself up stiff and straight, and in this very deep, loud voice said, "Sgt Major Foster, you, orrible slovenly bunch!"

Ellie shrieked. I said, "*Another* war movie?" I didn't mean to pour cold water on Dad's moment of triumph, but I sometimes wish they could make a few more movies about, well, love, for instance, instead of all this macho fighting stuff. But I could see Ellie starting to bristle – she is very protective towards Dad – so I hastily added that all I meant was he'd been in a war movie last time. "*Blaze of Glory?* That was all about war!"

"Yes, but that was practically just a walk-on," said Ellie. "He hardly got to say a line. This time he's got *dialogue*. Haven't you, Dad? You've got dialogue! Loads of it. He'll have his name in the credits. We can tell everyone to go and watch!"

"I could still end up on the cutting-room floor," said Dad; but I could see he was excited. A real part in a real movie! I was really pleased for him... until I discovered he was going to be abroad on location for almost the whole of the school holidays.

I wailed, "Oh, no! *Please!*"

Everyone looked at me in amazement. "What's the problem?" said Mum.

The problem was that Mum was also going to be away. *She* was going off on tour, with a play.

"Not the Aunties!" I said.

But I knew that it would be. We have these really complicated arrangements for what Mum calls "child care".

They try not to both be away during term time, but if they are it's usually not for very long and I always stay with Katie and Ellie stays with her friend Carla, up the road. Sometimes when we were little Dad's mum used to come and look after us, but she's in a home now, so if it's holiday time we get shipped off to the ancient old Aunties in Clacton. We almost never seem to have any money for proper holidays, like other people.

Mum seemed at a bit of a loss. "I thought you liked going to stay with the Aunties?"

"That was when I was younger," I said.

"You mean like last year?"

"Couldn't I stay with Katie?" I said. "Mum, please!"

"But what about Ellie? She'd be all on her own."

"No, she wouldn't! There's always Drew and Chelsea." Drew and Chelsea are kids who live next door to the Aunties. We'd been friends with them for years. But they are just kids. OK for Ellie; not for me.

Dad said, "Won't Katie be going off somewhere?"

Yes. Damn! She would. I hadn't thought of that.

"Maybe... " Mum glanced at Dad for confirmation. "Maybe we could offer to pay for Tamsin to go with Katie and her mum and dad? Wherever it is they're off to."

"No! I'd forgotten. They're going to America." I tried to quell the note of panic in my voice. I couldn't go to America! It would be even worse than Clacton. At least Clacton was in the same country. "It'd be way too expensive! It would make me feel guilty."

"Yes, and it wouldn't be fair," said Ellie.

"No, it wouldn't. It wouldn't be fair!"

"Not unless we *both* went."

"You can't go inviting yourself on someone's holiday," I said. And then it came to me: the perfect solution. "Beth! I could stay with Beth!" If I stayed with Beth I'd be able to see Alex every single day. Beth wouldn't nag to come with me, she had boyfriends of her own.

"Who's Beth?" said Mum.

"She's in my class, she's really nice! And *she* won't be going away, she never goes away. Her mum's even more broke than we are."

Dad winced slightly when I said this. Ellie shrilled, "We won't be broke now Dad's got a part in a movie!"

"Certainly not *as* broke," said Dad. "I'll tell you what... we'll all go off somewhere at Christmas. How about that?"

I didn't care about Christmas. Christmas was months away! I cared about *now*.

"Please!" I begged. "*Please* let me stay with Beth!"

Mum looked across at Dad. "What do you reckon?"

"We'll think about it," said Dad. "Not making any promises, mind!"

That was all right. I could get round them!

Alex wasn't working on the flats any more. They'd finished converting the house and moved to another job, several streets away. I really missed seeing him on the way to school in the morning, but at least he hadn't moved to the other side of town – or, worse still, another part of the country. I could still see him in the afternoon. I looked forward to it all day! Counting the hours, even the minutes, till I could be with him. Fortunately, Mum was up in town rehearsing for her tour and Dad was doing a play way over in Bromley, which meant neither of them was at home when me and Ellie got back from school. Ellie usually went up the road to Carla's, so nobody knew that I was getting off the bus four stops early and going to spend time with Alex.

One afternoon when I'd just got in, Mum rang to say she'd been invited to a party to meet some big TV director and wouldn't be back till late.

"Is that OK? Will you be all right by yourselves?"

I said we would be fine, and promptly rang Alex on his mobile. We arranged to meet in the Pamino Bar, in half an hour. The Pamino Bar had become our special place. It was small and poky but nobody seemed to mind how long we sat there. I told Ellie I was going round to Katie's.

She said, "*Again?* You're always going round to Katie's! I think you're lesbians. Either that or you're secretly meeting someone."

I looked at her, rather sharply. What did she know???

"Is that what you're doing? Secretly meeting someone?

It's all right, I won't tell Mum! Not if you confess."

I said, "There's nothing *to* confess. I'm going round to Katie's. And we are not lesbians, you little snot bag!"

She sulked at that. "You're supposed to be looking after me."

"That's all right, I won't be long. You can go back to Carla's for a couple of hours."

"I don't want to go back to Carla's! I want to stay here. You oughtn't to be going out and leaving me. Anything could happen! I could start a fire. I could have a heart attack. I could – "

"Oh, don't be so childish!" I said. "Let's go."

She refused, point blank. Just dug in her heels. She can be *really* obstinate. It gets me so mad!

"I don't see why I should have to go out just cos you are. Why can't Katie come round here?"

I snapped, "Because she can't! Just do as you're told."

"I won't. I'm staying here. And it'll be all your fault if you get back to find the house burnt down!"

I wouldn't normally have left her on her own, but

I couldn't resist the opportunity to see Alex. Every minute we had was precious! Anyway, it wasn't like she was really scared. She was just being awkward on purpose to annoy me.

I told Ellie that I would be back by eight o'clock. I really meant to be. I am not an irresponsible person! It's just that sitting there with Alex, all cuddling and cosy, I lost track of time. And then we wandered out into the mall, and the shops were still open cos of it being Thursday and late-night closing, and it was all busy and buzzy and throbbing with people, and how could I say that I had to go home?

Alex took my hand. "I glad you nice girl, not gold-digger."

I giggled at that; I couldn't help it. I said, "*Gold*-digger? Where'd you get that from?"

"I read some place. Is not right word?"

"Depends what you mean by it."

"What I mean... you not girl that only want money... fast car. Go clubbing. Some girl... that all they want. You not have money – poof!" He made a gesture. "Goodbye, see you, finish!"

"That's because all they care about is glitz," I said. "All I care about is just being with you!"

"This what I mean," said Alex. "This why I love you."

Oh, God... I went all melty. "I love you, too!" I said.

We paused for a moment, then went on our way, hand in hand. It was then that Beth appeared, coming out of Starbucks. With a boy, goes without saying! Beth is always with a boy. Her eyes widened when she saw me and Alex. Then she grinned, and waved, and called out, "Way to go!"

It would be all round school before first break...

I did feel a moment of panic when I saw the time on the big clock at the end of the mall: half past nine! Mum would be back before me if I weren't careful. I told Alex that I should have gone home ages ago.

"It's my little sister... she's on her own."

We ran all the way, Alex still holding my hand. But we didn't run fast enough, or maybe we shouldn't have stopped for a good-night kiss. Not that anything had happened; the house was still standing. But even as I tore panting round the corner, Mum was letting herself in at the front door...

CHAPTER FIVE

I got into quite a bit of trouble, going out and leaving Ellie on her own. Mum went on and on about it. *Ten years old, anything could have happened! Thought I could trust you. Obviously wrong.*

"What on earth were you thinking of?"

In vain I bleated that Katie and I were doing this

very important project for school. "I'm really sorry! We got carried away."

No use; Mum just wasn't buying it. She said it was the lamest excuse she'd ever heard and I ought to be ashamed of myself.

"Leaving your sister like that!"

"They're lesbians," said Ellie.

I said, "You shut up, turd features!"

Would you believe it? Mum had the nerve to tell me not to speak to my sister like that. *After what she'd just said to me.* I mean, it's pretty disgusting, coming from a ten-year-old. But Ellie is Mum's favourite, and Dad's too. Probably not surprising. She is *so* much more the right sort of daughter. At least she didn't go putting ideas into Mum's head by hinting at secret boyfriends. And, to be fair, she didn't actually gloat.

"I wouldn't have told her," she said, "if you'd got in a bit earlier… I knew she'd be mad at you!"

Mad was an understatement. Mum was still going on about it when we got up next morning. She told Dad, and he went on about it too. I thought they'd never stop.

"I'm just so disappointed in you," said Mum.

Mum wasn't the only one to be disappointed; Mrs Hendricks was, too. She is our history teacher, and I am definitely one of her favourites. History is my best subject. I always come top and get good marks for my homework. Never less than an A-. I can't help it, I am just naturally enthusiastic when it comes to dates and stuff. Even *boring* stuff, like the Corn Laws. I try to think what it must have been like for the poor, not being able to afford bread to feed their children, and that kind of makes it come alive. Mrs Hendricks is used to me sitting there all bright and earnest and boffinlike, ready to answer any question she throws at us. She knows she only has to say "Tamsin?" and I'll leap into action. Except this time I didn't, cos this time I was sitting there in class dreaming about Alex.

When Mrs Hendricks said, "Tamsin? Date of the first Corn Law?" my mind was like a total blank. Just a ball of cotton wool. She was expecting it of me. I made a wild guess.

"1904?"

There was a pause, then somebody tittered. Then other people tittered. Apparently it was a really stupid answer. So stupid that even a dumbo like Kyle Mellish, who spent most of every class picking his nose and flicking bits of snot at people, was honking and snorting. I'd obviously made a complete idiot of myself. Mrs Hendricks raised an eyebrow and said, "Katie?"

"1804," said Katie.

I was only, like, a hundred years out. Mrs Hendricks said, "Thank you, that's better. I'm surprised at *you*, Tamsin."

I felt bad about that. I felt that I'd let her down. Afterwards I thought, well, if I'd said 1904 and it was really 1804 that showed I had actually known, I'd just had a moment of confusion. I still felt bad; but I still went on dreaming about Alex. Sometimes I got so lost in my world of make-believe I hardly knew what was going on around me. Mr McCarthy, our maths teacher, came and banged on my desk one day, so loud it made me jump.

"TAMSIN MITCHELL," he thundered, "ARE YOU STILL WITH US?"

It was a rude awakening. You can get really lost in daydreams.

"If you *are* with us might I ask that you devote a modicum of attention to my maths lesson? Just a modicum. Or is that perhaps too much of an imposition?"

"Too much!" yelled Kyle, growing excited. Like he even knows what an imposition *is*.

Beth, who is often quite cheeky with teachers and seems to get away with it, said, "You'll have to forgive her, sir… she's in love!"

Of course I went bright scarlet; but I couldn't help a glow of pride, spreading like warm treacle through my body. I was in love! And everybody knew it.

"Who is he?" demanded Beth at breaktime. A little gaggle had clustered round me, all eager to hear the details. "I saw her with him," said Beth. "In the mall. They were like all lovey dovey." She grabbed someone's hand and started planting kisses on her cheek. "Mwah, mwah!"

I protested, a bit feebly. "We weren't doing that. Not when you saw us."

"Hah!" Beth turned triumphantly, and pointed a finger in my face. "That's an admission! That means you *had* been doing it. Or were *going* to do it. And don't say you weren't cos I won't believe you!"

By now I was all lit up like a Christmas tree. Beth said, "Ooh, look! She's embarrassed!"

Oonagh Fox, the girl whose hand she'd grabbed, told Beth to lay off. "We're still waiting to hear who he is! Is he at this school?"

I said, "No, he's left school. He's seventeen."

"Wow!" Beth studied me with new respect. "You're a dark horse!"

Who'd have thought it? The boring old boffin, having a real proper boyfriend.

"Where'd you meet him?"

Katie got in ahead of me. "On a *building* site," she said.

Beth stuck her fingers up. "Shut up, snobby! What's wrong with that?"

Nothing! I looked at her, gratefully. I felt a bit sorry for Katie, but really she had asked for it. "He's Polish," I said. "He doesn't speak much English."

"Ah!" Beth nodded, wisely.

"That explains it… if you can't talk… " She kissed the air noisily.

Oonagh said, "Who wants to talk, anyway?"

"Yeah, right! Not what boys are for." Beth gave me a companiable biff on the shoulder.

"Go for it, girl!"

They were treating me like I was one of them. Like at long last I'd joined the club.

Katie said to me, as we went back into school, that she thought Beth was wrong. "Boys aren't just for kissing! I wouldn't want a boy I couldn't talk to."

I said, "We do talk!"

"About what?" said Katie.

"Everything! Anything!" I could see she was about to start challenging me, like *how can you talk when he doesn't even speak English,* but I really didn't want us to start fighting again. Quickly, changing the subject, I said, "Have you done your essay for Mrs Martinez yet?" Doing my best to sound like I cared.

Katie gave me that look that she does when she can't quite believe what she's hearing. She said, "What do you mean, have I done it? They were due to be handed in on Monday."

Oh, God, oh, God! And I hadn't even started. Where had I been???

"You know what?" said Katie. "You're losing it!"

She was right. My schoolwork was going down the tubes, fast. Even when I remembered to do my homework I wasn't getting my usual marks. When did I ever get a B- for anything??? Never! Next week was Open Evening for Year 8. Mum would dutifully be coming along to chat with the teachers and get a progress report, and Dad, too, if his play had finished. I'd lost all track of what was happening in the outside world. But anyway, Mum by herself would be bad enough.

"I don't know what's come over Tamsin just lately."

I could hear all of them - Mrs Hendricks, Mrs Martinez, Mr McCarthy. "Her grades are slipping, she's not concentrating, I'm really worried about her."

I should probably have been worried too, but I wasn't. I was on a rollercoaster. I didn't have time to worry! I was already making plans for the summer. I spoke to Beth one day when we were alone in the girls' toilets, and she said I could stay at her place as long as I liked, no problem.

"I'll tell my mum, she won't mind. Probably won't even notice you're there! Doesn't even notice I'm there, half the time. We'll have a laugh, it'll be great!"

In spite of the telling-off I'd had about leaving Ellie on her own, I was still getting off the bus four stops early every afternoon to go and see Alex. Sometimes we just had time for a chat or a quick kiss and a cuddle – in full view of anyone who happened to walk by. I didn't care! When Alex put his arms round me it was like we were enclosed in our own private world. Other times we walked up the road to a tiny little park and wandered round in the sunshine until it was time for me to go. I worried that Alex would think it really babyish of me, always having to get back, not being able to stay out late, so I told him that Mum and Dad were really old-fashioned.

"They treat me like a *child*."

"Is all right," said Alex. "I understand. They want keep you safe." And then he said, "You ask if OK Saturday you come with us have meal somewhere? Me, you, Marek, Marta? Marta want meet you." He grinned. "I tell her bout you. I say you very sweet girl, very pretty. Beautiful eyes."

I melted when he said that. I'm *not* pretty, but I have always been proud of my eyes. They are definitely my best feature.

"Like sea," said Alex. "Marta she nice girl. She and Marek, they an item." He folded his arms round me. "I want be an item with you, Tamsin! You want be an item with me?"

I nodded ecstatically, not trusting myself to speak.

"Then that it," said Alex. "We an item... you, me. Together! Right?"

I said, "Right!"

"So you ask your mum if OK Saturday, OK?"

Recklessly, I told him that I didn't need to. "It'll be fine!"

"We're going bowling," I told Beth, next day at school. "Then afterwards we're going somewhere for a meal."

I waited anxiously for her approval. She nodded. "Cool!"

"Have you ever been bowling?"

"Yeah, it's fun."

"But is it difficult?" I'm not very good at sports. I desperately didn't want to seem silly and babyish.

Beth said, "Don't worry, you'll get the hang of it. Not like it really matters, anyway."

"How d'you mean?" I stared at her doubtfully.

"Well, come on!" She gave me a little knowing nudge in the ribs. "Who cares?"

"Thing is... I have this problem!" The words came bleating out of me. I felt I could confess to Beth and that she would understand.

"What's that?" she said.

"I haven't told my parents!"

"About what?"

"About going out with Alex."

"Oh." She looked at me, with sudden interest. "Wouldn't they approve?"

I said, "You know what parents are like."

"I know what my mum's like," said Beth. "Too busy going out with her own boyfriends to check who I go out with. Shouldn't have thought yours'd be the sort to get fussed."

It is true that Mum and Dad are quite free and easy compared to, say, Katie's mum and dad, who have these really rigid rules about television, for instance, and the internet. We don't have any form of censorship in our house; Mum and Dad don't believe in it. So long as we *talk*. But I wasn't talking! I was deliberately deceiving them. But I knew, deep inside me, that talking wouldn't make any difference. They still wouldn't be happy about me going out with Alex.

I said this to Beth, who shook her head wonderingly. She said, "What's to object to?"

I said, "Just about everything." The fact that Alex was sixteen, the fact that I hadn't told them. The fact that he'd smiled at me when he was working on the buildings. The fact that I'd smiled back… I heaved a sigh. "I don't know what to do! If I tell them, they'll want to meet him."

"So?"

"So then he'd discover how old I was!"

"You mean – " Beth's eyes lit up. "He doesn't know?"

Miserably I shuffled my feet. "He thinks I'm nearly sixteen."

"Cool!" She laughed. "It's not like everyone could get away with it. Not that you *behave* like you're nearly sixteen… but looks-wise you might just pass. Just about."

I knew she meant it as a compliment, and that I ought to feel flattered. "But what do I do about Saturday?" I wailed. "What am I going to tell them?"

"What d'you usually tell them?"

"I usually say I'm going round to Katie's, but then they expect me to be back by half past eight."

"Half past *eight*?"

"Well, or if I'm going to be later they want to come and pick me up."

"Ah. Mm. I see." Beth crinkled her forehead. "I see the problem."

"I can't tell Alex I've got to be back by half past eight! Not if we're going for a meal."

"No, you can't," said Beth. "Not if you're supposed to be nearly sixteen. That'd be ridiculous! You could always say you're spending the night at Katie's, then go back and stay with Alex instead. Go home in the morning... they wouldn't know!"

They wouldn't. But... "Stay with Alex?" I said.

"Why not?" She cackled happily. "You're nearly sixteen!"

I kept thinking about what Beth had said. Stay with Alex... well, and why not? It was the perfect solution. That way I wouldn't need to be a silly little baby and start bleating about having to go home. Nobody who was nearly sixteen had to be home by eight thirty on a

Saturday night! It was pathetic. I would be far too ashamed.

I knew where Alex lived. He and Marek shared a room in one of the old crumbling houses out near Western Way, the other side of town. He'd never let me visit as he said it wasn't nice.

"Marek, he very untidy… very dirty person."

But if I told him Mum and Dad had to be up *really* early for work, and wouldn't thank me for thumping about the house at eleven o'clock at night… it wasn't a total lie! Sometimes when they're filming they do have to be up at the crack of dawn.

"It would just make it easier." That was what I would say.

To my surprise, Alex was quite shocked. He said he couldn't possibly let me stay with him, it wasn't right.

"If it's because of Marek," I said, "I don't mind untidiness!"

Frankly, I live in a house that is full of mess and clutter. Stuff all over the place. I am the only one in the family who likes a bit of order, the rest are just litter bugs.

I said this to Alex, but he wouldn't budge. I had never known him be so stubborn before. Usually I could get him to do whatever I wanted. Very firmly he said that he would take me home at the end of the evening and I would let myself in at the front door "very quiet like a leetle mouse" and go on "toe tip" up the stairs, not to disturb Mum and Dad.

Sadly, but a bit proudly as well, I reported back to Beth. "He doesn't think it would be right."

"What is this guy?" said Beth. "Your father or your boyfriend?"

I said, "He's my boyfriend, and he loves me!"

I thought for a minute she was going to make some kind of jeering retort, but after a pause she said, "Well, think yourself lucky! I wouldn't mind a boyfriend like that."

Eagerly I said, "Anyway, it's all right cos I know what I'm going to do... I've got a plan!"

"Good for you," said Beth. "Hope it works out OK."

It would! It was foolproof; there was nothing that could go wrong.

Ten-pin bowling turned out to be fun even though, as I had suspected, I wasn't very good at it. I'd seen it so often in movies and it always looked so easy. A huge great ball... how could you possibly miss? Still, I wasn't the only one; Marek's girlfriend Marta wasn't all that much better. She kept crouching down really low and waggling her bum in the air like she knew what she was doing, but she hardly knocked down any more pins than I did. Not, as Beth had said, that it mattered. I think secretly the two boys enjoyed us being so useless as it meant they could show off. I was glad that Alex was good at it. I know it is very pathetically unfeminist of me, but I would far rather he was good and I was bad than the other way round.

Every now and again Marek and Marta would break off to kiss, so me and Alex did too. Marek kept teasing us, which I didn't really mind though I didn't see what right he had considering he was doing exactly the same thing. Marta went, "Tweet tweet! Little lovebirds!" and I didn't see what right she had either. To be honest, I wasn't too sure about Marta. She had yellow hair and black eyebrows, and she was wearing these really tight, bright pink Lycra leggings and a green top with bobbles on it, which I wouldn't have been seen dead in.

I know you shouldn't judge people by appearances but sometimes, I reckon, what you wear is what you *are*. I mean, we all choose our clothes to suit our personality. Marta was a quite loud, bossy sort of person, whereas I am just the opposite. I never choose stuff that will draw attention to me.

Still, if I thought Marta looked tacky she probably thought I looked boring, just wearing jeans and a T-shirt. She certainly treated me like I was boring. She was the only one who could speak proper English, but she hardly talked to me at all, just jabbered all the time in Polish, saying things that made Marek laugh. I had this feeling that it was me they were laughing about. Alex kept squeezing my hand as if to reassure me, and telling Marta to speak English.

We went upstairs afterwards for a meal. It was all American, so I had a hamburger and a milk-shake.

The others drank lager, which Marta insisted that I try. I had one sip, and they all laughed as I pulled a face.

Marta made another of her remarks, and Marek grinned. Alex said, "English! Speak English!"

Marta said, "No, let's teach Tamsin how to speak Polish. What shall we teach her? What will be of use to her? I know, I know! Tamsin, say to Alex... *koham chyeh*."

Well, that's what it sounded like. I repeated it obediently. "*Koham chyeh*."

Marta clapped her hands. "Good! And now you say... *ko-ash niyeh?*"

I hesitated. "What does it mean?"

"Just say it, say it! *Ko-ash niyeh?*"

I could feel my face starting to go tomato. I was sure she was making fun of me.

"No, is all right." Alex nodded gravely. "You say!"

Reluctantly, I mumbled it: "*Ko-ash nvyeh?*"

Alex said, "*Koham chyeh!*" and pulled me to him.

Then they told me what it meant. Marta wrote down the words for me:

Kochasz mnie? Do you love me?

Kocham çie, I love you

"Is the language of love," said Marek.

Very useful." Marek winked. "You learn!"

I am actually quite good at languages, especially French and Spanish, but Polish looked to me to be really difficult. I said, "What does this do?", pointing to the little symbol under the *c* of *çie*. "We don't have it in English. They have it in French. What's it called in Polish?"

They all looked at me blankly. "Does anyone care?" said Marta.

She obviously thought me some nerdy stuck-up geek. Why couldn't I have just kept my stupid mouth shut? Alex, tightening his arm round me, said, "She very clever girl. She know these things." But who wanted to be clever? In future, I was definitely going to think before I spoke.

On the way home Alex told me that Marta didn't believe I was nearly sixteen. "She say you look too young!" He laughed. "I tell her, she just jealous!"

I laughed too, but hoped it was the last time we would have to go out as a foursome.

It was eleven o'clock when we reached home. Alex was worried in case I was out later than I should have been, but I told him there was no problem: "I'm nearly sixteen!"

He reminded me to go on "toe tip" so as not to wake my parents. Then he kissed me and whispered, "I love you, Tamsin!"

I whispered back, "*Kocham çie!*"

He waited till I was at the front door, then blew me a last kiss and walked off, into the night. I knew the chain would be on the door and that there was no point trying my key in the lock. But I wasn't worried: I had it all worked out. Everything under control.

I pressed my finger on the bell – and that was when it all blew up in my face.

CHAPTER SIX

Almost before I had time to take my finger off the bell, the door was wrenched open and Mum was standing there, her face all scrunched and furious. I was somewhat taken aback but I wasn't worried; I had my story all worked out. Every detail. I'd been over and over it.

"*Where have you been?*" Mum hissed it at me.

She grabbed hold of my arm and yanked me inside. Dad had appeared, at the end of the hall.

He shouted, "Tamsin, is that you?" He sounded pretty angry. What was going on?

"Get in there!" Now it was Dad who was grabbing me. He hauled me down the hall and thrust me into the sitting room. Mum bundled after us. She closed the door and leaned against it, arms folded.

She said, "*Well?*"

I kept my cool; I gave them the story. "I've been at Katie's! I told you... I thought I was staying over, but her auntie and uncle were there so I couldn't, so her dad brought me home. He just dropped me off at the corner."

There was a silence. It sounded kind of... ominous.

Mum looked at Dad, Dad looked at Mum. It was like they were waiting to see which of them was going to be the first to say something. Growing desperate, I jumped in with both feet.

"I'm sorry, I should have rung you!"

There. Now I had apologised, and that should have been that. But it wasn't. Dad headed me off, as I made for the door. "Oh, no, you don't, young woman! You come back here."

"Look, I'm *sorry*," I said. "But I knew you wouldn't be worried. You knew where I was, so – "

"We rang Katie," said Mum.

What?

"I wanted to remind you... we need to leave early tomorrow."

Icy fingers clutched my heart.

"Tim and Megan?" said Mum. In this distinctly cold, unfriendly tone of voice. "We're all going over there for lunch?"

The icy fingers squeezed and palped. I swallowed a ping pong ball that was lodged in my throat. I'd forgotten about lunch.

"I spoke to Katie... she said you weren't there..." Mum paused obviously waiting for some kind of an explanation. But I didn't have one.

"She said you hadn't even made any arrangements to be there."

Katie could have lied. It wouldn't have hurt her. She could have said… *something*. I would have done. We were supposed to be friends!

"Tamsin, where have you been?" said Dad.

"More to the point," said Mum, "*who have you been with?*"

I froze; blood, bones, tongue, everything. It was like my whole body had turned into this big block of ice.

"Katie said you'd been seeing some Polish boy?"

She'd told them! She'd actually told them!

"Some Polish boy from a *building* site?"

I tried to think of something to say, but nothing came. Even if it had, I couldn't have said it. My tongue was a solid wodge that wouldn't move.

"Ellie says she's seen you talking to one of the boys up the road… the big house they've been turning into flats. She says you seemed quite friendly with one of them." Spying little *toad*. "Is he the one you were with?"

My heart hammered and pounded.

"Well?" said Dad. "*Is* he?"

Slowly and reluctantly, I nodded.

"So why for God's sake didn't you tell us? What's with all this creeping around behind our backs? Are we ogres? Are we unreasonable? Or is it because you knew full well you shouldn't be going out with him?"

My tongue suddenly sprang back to life. "Why shouldn't I be going out with him?"

"I don't know," said Dad. "You tell me."

"I can't, there isn't any reason!" I hurled it at them. "Just that you're so snobby!"

"I beg your pardon?" said Mum.

"Snobby. You are! You've just proved it... boy from a *building* site! Or maybe you'd like him to go and *sign on*, like an out-of-work actor!"

Dad ignored that crack. He said, "Stop being on the defensive, it just makes you seem all the more guilty. How old is this boy?"

"I don't know! Fifteen."

"*Fifteen?*" Mum looked at me, rather hard. "Ellie says more like twenty."

"He's nowhere near twenty!"

"But he's not fifteen, is he?"

"How would she know?"

"Tamsin, tell me the truth! *How old is he?*"

Sullenly I muttered, "Seventeen."

"I see." Mum breathed deeply. "Seventeen! So why did you feel the need to lie?"

"Cos I knew you'd get stupid about it!"

"Does he know how old you are?" said Dad.

"Yes! No."

"Which?"

"He doesn't know!" That at least was true. "We haven't talked about it."

"I find that hard to believe," said Dad.

"Well, we haven't! We don't *talk* about stupid things like how old we are. How old we are doesn't matter!"

"I'm sorry," said Dad, "but I'm afraid it does. Seventeen is far too old for someone your age."

Dad had some nerve! He is *fourteen years* older than Mum. Talk about double standards.

I said, "Why are you so hung up about age?"

"We're not hung up," said Mum. "Your dad's right. And I think in your heart of hearts you know it, otherwise why have you kept it from us?"

"Because I knew you'd be all snobby and make a fuss!"

"Now, you listen here, my girl." Dad pointed a finger in my face. "What we're *making a fuss* about is you going behind our backs and downright lying to us. Not to mention scaring the hell out of us! How do you think your mum and I felt when we discovered at half past nine at night that you weren't where you were supposed to be?"

"We've been having all kinds of nightmares," said Mum.

I said, "Well, I'm sorry, but you always treat us differently!"

There was a pause; then Mum said, "What are you talking about? Treat who differently?"

"Me and Ellie. You don't mind her having a boyfriend!"

"For heaven's sake, Tamsin, have a bit of sense! Obi's only ten years old."

"Yes, and you let them go out together!"

"We'd let you go out," said Dad, "if you had a boyfriend your own age. We don't object to you having a *boyfriend*. But seventeen is not a boy! It's a young man."

My heart swelled, even as he said it.

"What kind of seventeen-year-old goes out with a thirteen-year-old schoolgirl?"

"He must see, himself, that it's not appropriate," urged Mum.

I bristled at that. She could talk! She was the one who got married to my dad, that is my real dad, who she now **HATES**, on account of him walking out before I was hardly conscious. If it hadn't been for her being pregnant, they wouldn't ever have got married in the first place. How appropriate is *that*? Having to get married cos you're pregnant?

Dad said, "*seventeen!*" Like it was some kind of crime. "He's either completely naïve, or – "

Or *what?* "Why are you being so ageist?" They wouldn't be racist, or sexist. "Why pick on Alex just cos he happens to be a bit older?"

"Don't be ridiculous, we're not picking on him," said Mum.

"Dad is!" I choked. "He's being totally unreasonable!"

Dad said, "Yes, and guess what? He's going to be even more unreasonable! As far as I'm concerned, that's it. You've blown it. Enough is enough! I don't want you seeing this boy again."

I felt like shouting, "I thought you said he was a young man?" but I was suddenly feeling too shaken to say anything. Not see Alex *ever again?* I turned helplessly to Mum.

"Tamsin, I'm sorry," said Mum, "but you've brought it on yourself. We always thought we could trust you."

I said, "You can trust me!"

"After you've *lied* to us?" That was Dad, still thundering away.

"Tammy, why did you?" said Mum. She suddenly

sounded sorrowful and hurt. "I thought we had the sort of relationship where we could talk."

"She lied," said Dad, "because she felt guilty!"

I turned, and screamed at him. "I lied because I knew you'd be all snobby!"

"Now you're being unfair," said Mum. "It's nothing to do with being snobby! Just that once you're out at work, you start to grow up really fast. And anyway – " She broke off, and looked at me. "You still haven't told us how you actually met him."

Sullenly, cos I knew what the reaction would be, I muttered, "He ran into me with his wheelbarrow".

Dad made a loud noise of exasperation.

"He was very apologetic!" I said. "He was scared he might have hurt me."

"So then what happened?" said Mum.

"He asked me out."

"And you went? With a boy you knew absolutely nothing about?" Dad's face had turned all red and mottled, like when he was doing his sergeant major act.

"Exactly how long," he said, "has this been going on?"

I opened my mouth in protest. Nothing had been going on! But I wasn't quite brave enough to say it. I'd never known Mum and Dad in such a lather.

"I asked you a question!" roared Dad. "*How long?*"

I mumbled, "Just a few weeks."

Needless to say, that brought Dad crashing in again. "*Just a few weeks?* A few weeks of sneaking around behind our backs? A few weeks of telling lies?"

Desperately I protested that Alex didn't know. "It wasn't his fault! Mum, please... *please* don't make me stop seeing him!"

Mum shot a glance at Dad. I felt that left to herself she might waver, but Dad was horrendously angry. He said,

"I don't want any more discussion. Thanks to you we have just lived through the worst couple of hours of our entire lives! You are *not* seeing this boy again, and that is the end of it. Now get to bed!"

Ellie was waiting for me on the upstairs landing, crouched behind the banisters in her nightdress. She whispered, "What happened? Where have you been? I heard Dad shouting."

I hissed, "You had to go and *tell*, didn't you?"

"I didn't! I didn't tell anything! I just said I'd seen you talking to this boy."

"Yes, well, thank you very much!" I said.

Next day I got Mum on her own in the kitchen and pleaded desperately with her. "Tell Dad he can't dictate like this!"

"He's not dictating," said Mum. "We both feel the same way. You really scared the life out of us, you know."

"I won't do it again, I promise!"

"Well," said Mum, "*do* you promise? Do I have your word that you won't attempt to see this boy again?"

That wasn't what I'd meant! All I'd meant was that I wouldn't scare them again.

"I'm waiting," said Mum.

"Mum, I can't," I wailed, "I can't! I love him – and he loves me! I can't not see him!"

"Oh, Tammy." Mum sighed. "I know what it's like

to be young and in love, believe me, I do. But your dad is right. However nice he is, this boy is far too old for you. You're far too young for him! For both your sakes we have to put a stop to it."

"But how can I just not see him any more? He'd be so hurt, he wouldn't know what was happening!"

"If you like," said Mum, "if it makes it any easier, you can give him a call and tell him to come round, and I'll have a word with him. It's all right, I'll treat him gently! I won't let your dad get at him."

I was torn. I felt that if Mum could just meet Alex she would see for herself what a sweet person he was. She would see that he wasn't any danger! On the other hand, she would discover that I'd told him I was nearly sixteen, and that would just totally freak her. It would confirm Dad's worst suspicions.

"Couldn't I at least see him one last time?" I begged. "Just so I can tell him myself?"

Mum hesitated.

"Please, Mum?"

"I'd really rather you didn't actually see him," said Mum. "Couldn't you just telephone?"

I told her that phoning was no good. "He doesn't speak much English. It's hard for him to understand."

"Well... all right! Just this one last time. But it had better not be while your dad's here." Dad at that moment was shut away in the sitting room, practising his lines. We could hear his sergeant major bellow shaking the house.

"I could slip out really quickly and get back," I said.

"No. Your dad might ask where you've gone. I don't want to take a leaf out of your book and start lying to him. He loves you just as much as he loves Ellie, you know. He was nearly going out of his mind last night, thinking something had happened to you."

I said again that I was sorry.

"Yes, well, sorry doesn't really cut it," said Mum. "You can think yourself lucky I'm giving you this one last chance. Where do you usually meet him?"

I muttered that he was working just a few streets away.

"Right, well, I suggest you drop by on your way back from school on Monday and explain the situation to him. I shall be here," said Mum. "I shall expect you home no later than four thirty. Is that understood?"

I nodded.

"Good. Well, don't let me down. I'm trusting you."

I didn't let Mum down: I got home by four thirty. Mum said, "Good girl!" and hugged me.

"So." She held me at arm's length, anxiously studying my face. "Is everything all right?"

I hunched a shoulder.

"You explained that you couldn't see him any more?"

Angrily I pulled away from her. "That's what you wanted, isn't it?"

Mum said, "Oh, Tammy, don't be like that! I know you hate me right now, but try to see things from our point of view. We're your parents, we're responsible for you!"

"I don't want to talk about it." I swiped a packet of biscuits out of the cupboard and made for the door.

"I'm going upstairs to do my homework."

"Well, don't stay up there all night," said Mum. "Come down and be sociable!"

I made a grunting noise.

"*Please?*" said Mum.

I gave another grunt; I wasn't making any promises. I *hadn't* made any promises. And I hadn't told any lies! *You explained,* Mum had said, *that you couldn't see him any more?* I hadn't properly answered her. I really didn't *want* to tell any more lies. I would if I had to. But only if I had no choice. I'm not naturally an untruthful person; I bet Ellie has told Mum and Dad far more whoppers than I have. I'd told Alex that we had to talk. We'd wandered up the road to the park, and sat on a bench, holding hands. Alex hadn't wanted to talk; he'd just wanted to kiss and cuddle. We hadn't seen each other for three whole days, and it seemed like a lifetime. But we needed to be serious.

"Listen," I said, "I know it's a drag, but – *stop it.*" I pushed at him. "I'm trying to *talk.*"

He said, "I don't want talk!"

"I can't help it, we've got to. *Listen*. Stop it! This is important."

He corrected me. "*This* what important!"

As best I could, with my lips squashed against his, I said, "Yes-and-we-won't-be-able-to-do-it-again-for-a-whole-week!"

That stopped him. He said, "Why? You go way?"

"No, it's my mum and dad getting all fussed about exams." In fact we'd already had exams. We hadn't had any results, but I was pretty sure that for the first time ever I wouldn't have come top of anything. It didn't bother me in the least little bit. Exams just didn't seem that important any more.

Alex said, "Why your mum and dad get fussed?"

"Oh, cos that's what they do! They *fuss*. They think I'm not working hard enough. They expect me to stay in every night and study and go to bed early. It's only just for this one week!"

After that Mum would be off on tour and Dad

would be away on location and I would be staying with Beth. She'd confirmed that it would be OK. "No problemo!" We'd agreed that we'd have fun together, going out as a foursome, me and Alex, Beth and whichever boy she happened to be seeing.

Alex pulled a face and said that a week was a long time. I said, "Yes, but then it's holidays and we can see each other every single night! It's just this hang-up they've got about *education*." I groaned, to show that I didn't have any hang-ups. I could feel the shadow of Katie, looming disapprovingly at my shoulder. I shrugged it off. "They want me to go on to uni. *University*."

"Ah. Uni." Alex nodded. "You very clever girl."

"Not that clever." I didn't want to come across as a total boring swot. "What about you? D'you think you might go to uni some day?"

He looked alarmed. He said, "Me?"

"Once you've learnt enough English … you could! We could go together."

He shook his head at that. He said he wasn't clever enough. "Always at school – " He pointed his thumb downwards. "No good!"

"So what d'you think you'll do," I said, "in the end?"

"What I do in the end... I be my own boss!" He laughed. "I be like Stefan!"

Stefan was the man that he and Marek worked for.

"You could start your own company," I said. "Be a company director!"

"Yes, I be company director. The boss! I tell people what they do... and they better damn do it, or else!"

"You might end up with a whole empire," I said.

"I be millionaire. Live in big house. Smoke cigar. Drive fast car!"

I thought, at least Mum couldn't say he didn't have ambitions. And anyway, *she* hadn't gone to uni. Neither had Dad. And in spite of everything I'd never actually promised I wouldn't see Alex any more. Dad had *told* me I wasn't to; but I hadn't promised anything!

And now we had the whole of the summer holidays to

look forward to… no mum, no dad. No more creeping around, no more inventing stories. We could be together as much as we wanted!

CHAPTER SEVEN

"You promised me!" I screamed at Mum across the room. "You said I could!"

"Actually," said Mum, "we said we'd think about it. Your dad specifically said *no promises*."

"But I've arranged it all! Beth's already asked her mum. She's looking forward to it! *Why* can't I stay with her?"

"I'd just rather you didn't," said Mum.

"Why *not?*"

"Because a) I don't know her, b) I don't know her mum, and c) the temptation might prove too much for you."

I said, "What temptation?"

"I think you know the answer to that! I don't want to be worrying all the time, wondering what you're up to."

"You mean, you don't trust me!"

"Tamsin, you're still only thirteen."

"*You don't trust me!*"

"You haven't really given us much reason to, have you?" said Mum. "Sneaking out behind our backs... and now your school work is starting to suffer."

I might have known she'd bring that up. She and Dad had both gone to Open evening: they'd come home looking grim. Everyone had complained about me, and my exam results had been disastrous – well, compared with what they normally were. Mum didn't actually *say*, "You may not be as bright and pretty as your sister, but at least you've always done well at school." Still, I knew that was what she was thinking. I guess all parents like their kids to do *something* they can be proud of. Now I wasn't doing anything. Instead of "Tamsin always comes top, Tamsin always gets good marks," it would be, shock horror, "Tamsin's been seeing this really unsuitable boy!"

"I'd just feel easier in my mind," said Mum, "if you were with the Aunties."

She meant if I were banished. Shunted off to Clacton, miles away from Alex. A sort of desperation came over me. She couldn't do this! She was ruining my life!

Mum prattled on, happily oblivious of the volcano of rage that was boiling up inside me. "You can spend the last week of term with Katie. I've spoken to her mum." Warned her, more like. *Keep her under house arrest. Don't let her out of your sight.* "She'd love to have you there."

"So would Beth's mum! And I could be with Beth the whole summer!"

"Tamsin, we've just been through all this. Your dad and I don't need the aggravation! Try thinking of someone other than yourself, for a change. This movie could be your dad's big break — "

I said, "Yeah, yeah! Heard it all before."

I could tell at once that I'd got to her. In this tight, controlled voice she said, "What exactly do you mean by that?"

"Everything's always going to be the big break! Yours, Dad's, every time you get a part in anything, *this could be the big break*. Only it never is! You go off and leave us all for *nothing*. You're just totally irresponsible! Katie's mum and dad aren't always rushing off to do their own thing and dumping her on people. How d'you think it feels, always being dumped? Like that time you left us with your *agent*, it was *hideous*. And then the time we went to Tim and Megan, and they hadn't got the faintest idea, they obviously didn't want us there, but you and Dad were off *getting the big break* so we had to be *dumped*. Now it's the Aunties, for the whole of the summer! Other people go on holiday. Not us! We just get dumped on people… here, you take them! We're *actors*.

We can't be expected to look after them. I don't know why you ever had kids in the first place," I yelled, "except of course that I was a *mistake*!"

There was a long, rather dreadful silence. I knew I'd gone too far. But so had Mum! She'd brought it on herself. *She* was the one who was always boasting how she'd won a prize at drama school for playing Juliet in *Romeo and Juliet*. Hadn't it taught her anything? You can't forcibly separate people who are in love.

Quietly Mum said, "Is that really how you feel, or is it just the anger speaking?"

I shouted that it was really how I felt; then I burst into tears and ran from the room.

Later, Dad came to speak to me. He said, "You've really upset your mum. You know that? You've really hurt her. She's even speaking of pulling out of the play. At this late stage! That would get her into a whole load of trouble. Word gets round in this business... nobody wants to employ an unreliable actor."

I hunched a shoulder and mumbled. Dad looked at me

reproachfully. "Have you any idea how much this part means to her? Have you any idea how *important* it is? Blanche duBois is a part to die for! It's a dream come true. It's her big chance!"

"Big break," I said.

"Yes! And thanks to you, she's seriously thinking of giving it up. Well, she's not going to," said Dad, "because I'm not going to let her. I've already promised we'll do something at Christmas. We'll go off somewhere, all four of us. What more do you want?"

I thought, by Christmas they'd probably both be in panto and we'd all end up in Hull, or Middlesbrough. That would be exciting. *Big joke.* Not that I cared about Christmas. Who knew if I'd even be around by then? Wild schemes were already bobbing and bouncing like ping-pong balls in my head.

"I think," said Dad, "that it would be nice if you told your mum you were sorry."

But I wasn't! And I didn't care any more whether she went off on her stupid tour or stayed at home. *I had a plan.*

A few minutes after Dad had said his piece, Ellie came bursting in. Even she wanted to have a go at me.

"Why have you been so mean to Mum?" she said. "Poor Mum! She was so looking forward to playing Blanche! This could be her *big break*."

I said, "Yeah, like this time next year we could have world peace."

"Don't be so horrible! You're horrible! You don't know what it's like. I know how she feels cos I feel the same way. I want to be an actor more than anything else in the world, and there isn't anything that's going to stop me!"

There wasn't anything that was going to stop me being with Alex. Nobody, but *nobody*, was going to come between us.

The day she was due to go off on tour – which was the day I was going to Katie's – Mum did her best to make things up between us. I hadn't *exactly* not been speaking to her; but my demeanour was frosty. I just love that word!

Demeanour. I know it only means the same as behaviour, but it is somehow so much more dignified. *I* was being dignified. Cool and aloof to show my displeasure.

In the kitchen, as I munched on cornflakes, Mum pleaded with me not to go off in a huff. She looked so forlorn that I almost caved in and forgave her. But then I reminded myself that she was an actor; you couldn't necessarily go by the way she looked. She and Ellie, they hammed it up all the time. I also reminded myself that if she had her way I wouldn't ever see Alex again. A thought which made my *blood run cold.* So I hardened my heart and munched on in silence, shovelling cornflakes into my mouth.

"Maybe when your dad and I get back," said Mum, "we'll review the situation… see how you feel then."

See if you've grown out of this silly teenage obsession. That was what she *meant.*

"Dad's waiting for me," I said. He was driving me over to Katie's to dump my stuff. "Gotta go!" I picked up my bag, gave Mum a quick peck on the cheek and headed for the door.

"Tamsin!" She called after me. "Don't forget ... I'm trusting you!"

It was what Katie said to me later the same day, when we were walking round the playing field together during first break: "She's *trusting* you."

"That's her problem! I didn't ask to be trusted. I didn't make any promises!"

"But she's your mum," said Katie.

So what? She might be my mum, but Alex was my boyfriend, and I loved him! I said this, very forcibly, to Katie.

"I'm in love! Don't you understand? I have to see him! I can't just disappear without telling him where I'm going. I don't even know why I'm bothering to discuss it with you, anyway!"

"Cos I'm responsible for you," said Katie.

What?

"Well, my mum is. Which means I am, too, in a way."

"You mean my mum went and told your mum about Alex! She told her to make sure we didn't meet!"

Katie looked shifty. "Not exactly."

"What, then?"

"She didn't have to tell her! My mum already knew, cos of your mum ringing up that time thinking you were with me when you weren't."

I looked at her through narrowed eyes. I felt betrayed. This was supposed to be my best friend! "Are you saying if I don't get back from school the exact same minute you get back, your mum's going to start coming on all heavy?"

"She might ask where you are," said Katie. "Then what do I say?"

"Same as you said before, probably, when you told Mum I was going out with a boy from a *building* site."

Katie flushed. I could see I'd made her uncomfortable, and I was glad. She deserved to be uncomfortable!

"I had to tell her, I couldn't help it. She was worried! She thought something awful had happened to you. I'm sorry! But what else could I do?"

"You could make up for it," I said. "You could let me

go and see Alex after school today and not say anything to your mum."

"But what if she asks me?"

"She won't, cos she won't know!"

"Why won't she know?"

"Cos I'll be back home before she is, and if I'm not – well! You can just say I had to stay late."

"Why?" said Katie. "What'd you be staying late for?"

"I don't know! Think of something."

She scrunched up her face.

"What's the problem? You think I'm going to run away with him or something?"

That alarmed her. "Tamsin, you wouldn't!" she said.

"I might, if this goes on. But I'm not going to do it *today*. I'm not going to do it this week! Just if – "

"If what?"

"Nothing! Forget I said it." I wished I hadn't; I wasn't sure, any more, how much my best friend could be trusted. "Just do this one thing for me, then I won't ever ask you to do anything else. On my honour! Cross my heart and hope to die… just this one last thing!"

I honestly thought that would get to her. But Katie has these hugely high principles.

"I just don't want to have to lie to Mum," she said.

"You won't have to lie to her! I'll be home before she gets there! What time does she get in?"

Miserably Katie said, "I dunno… 'bout five o'clock."

"So I'll be back before. That is a *promise*. I don't break promises!"

She looked at me like she didn't believe me.

"If you're thinking that I promised Mum, I didn't. I wouldn't! Even if I had, it'd be like under duress. Like when they torture people. So it wouldn't count, anyway!"

Katie heaved a deep sigh. "I don't know what's happening to you," she said.

I spent the rest of the day counting the minutes till I could be with Alex. I sat through double maths decorating my rough book with hearts and flowers, writing his name over and over in different styles:

Alex Kozlowski

Alex Kozlowski

ALEX KOZLOWSKI

ALEX KOZLOWSKI

Then I wrote *Tamsin Kozlowski,* and *Mrs Tamsin Kozlowski,* and *Mr and Mrs Alex Kozlowski.* Katie, sitting next to me, watched without comment, but I could sense the waves of disapproval. I could understand that it was difficult for her, me being in love and her not having anyone, but Beth's reaction was *so* much more satisfying.

"That's her boyfriend," Beth said, pointing to my rough book, as we packed our bags at the end of maths. "He's Polish. Alex – " She peered closer. "Koz… how d'you pronounce it? Koz-*low*-ski?"

I told her, Koz-*lov*-ski.

"Kozlovski." She rolled her tongue round it. "Cool!"

I said, "Yes, but what's not so cool is Mum and Dad sending me away so's I can't meet up with him during the holidays."

Beth agreed that was a bummer. "We'd have had a really great time."

Katie said, "That's why her mum couldn't trust her."

"Oh, shut up, misery!" Beth shouldered past, on her way to the door. "Wittering on like some stupid old woman."

Katie went bright red. I felt ashamed for her and had to turn away. But then I felt ashamed of being ashamed and turned back again to try and comfort her, only she wouldn't let me; just shook me off and went marching out of the room. We made up later, cos we're never cross with each other for long, but I knew that she was still upset.

I didn't hang around at the end of school. I was first out of the classroom and first out of the gates, steaming up the road to the bus stop. I'd sent Alex a text, so he knew that I was coming. He was there waiting for me. As he saw me pounding round the corner he dropped the bucket he was carrying and raced towards me.

Dimly I was aware of Marek in the background,

grinning and winking like he always did, but I'd got used to Marek by now. He didn't bother me any more. What bothered me was having to break it to Alex that not only couldn't I see him later that evening, I couldn't see him for the whole of the rest of the summer.

"It's my mum and dad," I said. "They think I'm too young to be serious about anyone. It's just pathetic! They are so out of touch."

"What do we do?" he said. "Tamsin, I love you! What must we do?"

"I know what we do," I said. "End of August, I'm going to be sixteen – " I was almost starting to believe my own fantasy. "Once I'm sixteen I can do what I like. They can't stop me. We can run away together!"

"You mean – " He looked at me doubtfully. Obviously not sure whether he had quite understood.

"Run away! Why not?" People did it all the time. "We could go abroad, we could go to Spain! It's lovely there, lovely and warm. And now Poland's in the EU, you can go wherever you want!"

"But I not speak Spanish!"

"That's all right," I said. "I do. I can teach you. It's much easier than Polish. You'll pick it up in no time!"

He seemed a bit dazed. He said, "What we do there? In Spain?"

"Just be together," I said.

"Together. Yes!" He closed his arms round me. "I want be together… I want be with you always! But how we live?"

Of course, we would need money; even I could see that. I hadn't actually thought that far ahead. But in a flash, the answer came to me.

"You could start your own business! Be your own boss, just like you wanted. And I could help with the books!"

Alex seemed confused. "We going write books?"

"No!" I laughed, and he shook his head.

"I not understanding well."

"*Account* books." I could help with the books, and take telephone messages, and made appointments. Alex and I would work together! We would be partners. And we would make LOADS AND LOADS OF MONEY. Far more than Mum and Dad had ever made. That would show them!

Alex said, "You really think this good idea?"

"It's either that or not seeing each other any more. If you can live without seeing me – "

"No!" His arms tightened round me. "I love you, Tamsin!"

"And I love you. I can't live without you."

From somewhere behind us, Marek made one of those silly whey-hey type noises that boys sometimes make, thinking they're being funny. We ignored him.

"Why I not come speak with your mum and dad?" urged Alex. "Show them I not such a bad person."

"They're not here," I said. "Mum's on tour and Dad's filming. That's why they're sending me away."

"So when they back… I come see them. We talk."

I shook my head. "There wouldn't be any point." I couldn't have them finding out that I'd told lies about how old I was. I couldn't have *Alex* finding out. "They're very old-fashioned," I said bitterly.

"But when you sixteen – "

"It won't make any difference! I told you, they're stupid. Just stupid, *stupid*! They'll never let us be together."

"But – "

"Can't you understand?" In my desperation, I shrieked it at him. "They don't want me seeing you any more! Ever!"

"Tamsin." Alex tilted my face towards him. "Tamsin, don't cry! I love you so much. We do what you say... we be together!"

CHAPTER EIGHT

Before we kissed goodbye – our last kiss for six whole weeks – I said that we should take pictures of each other on our mobile phones. We had never bothered before; it didn't seem necessary, while we were together. But now we were going to be apart, and I almost couldn't bear it.

"If we don't have pictures we'll have nothing to remind us of each other!"

Alex said he didn't need a picture to remind me of him. "I am thinking of you all day."

I told him that I was thinking of him all day too. "But six weeks is such a long time! I want to have your photo so I can see it last thing at night before I go to sleep and first thing in the morning as soon as I wake up… *please!*"

It is a sad fact that I am *not* photogenic. I hate photos of me! They always make me look horse-faced and my hair all scraggly. When I saw the result on Alex's phone, I almost began to wish I hadn't insisted.

Alex said, "Nice!"

"It's not nice," I said, "it's horrible. Get rid of it!"

I snatched at his phone, but he laughed and held it away from me. "I need picture to remind me!"

"You said you didn't."

"I change my mind. Why you not like it?"

"It makes me look *ugly.*"

"Tamsin, you not ugly!" He sounded quite shocked.

"Well, I'm not *pretty*," I said.

Still holding the phone firmly out of reach, Alex squinted at the photo. "You have beautiful eyes," he said.

I glowed a bit at that. But it would still be nice to be photogenic. Mum and Ellie both are, even when you catch them off guard doing something silly, like pulling faces or letting their mouths drop open.

I sighed and said, "I s'pose it'll have to do. And I s'pose I'd better be going."

"I have present for you," said Alex.

Marek, who was still hovering nearby, looked across and grinned. "We get raise," he said. "More money. He spend it all on you!"

I asked Marek if he'd spent his on Marta, but he said no way. "She earn more than both of us."

Alex reappeared from indoors. "Here!" He pressed something into my hands.

"Oh!" My face immediately turned stupidly crimson. I am not very good at accepting gifts. *Or* compliments. I never know what to say. "You shouldn't have," I stammered.

"Please! You take." He closed my hands over it. "But not to open now. To open when home."

I couldn't wait that long. I clawed it open as soon as I was on the bus going back to Katie's. He'd bought me the most beautiful silver chain with a cluster of little blue stars. Really sweet! I put it on immediately, vowing to myself that I would never take it off, not even for school. We are not actually allowed to wear jewellery at school, but I reckoned I would find some way of hiding it. One thing was for sure, *I was not going to be parted from it.* It was like a little piece of Alex that would always be with me, even when we were miles away from each other.

Katie noticed it as soon as she opened the door. "Oh," she said, "that is so pretty!" And then she scowled and said, "Did he give it to you?"

I said, "Yes, he got a raise and he spent it all on me! I think it's real silver."

Scornfully Katie curled her lip. "You're joking! They sell those things down the market, I've seen them. They only cost about a tenner."

It's not like Katie to be mean, and I think she regretted it the minute she'd said it, cos she at once added that it didn't really matter if it were silver or not, it was the *thought* that counted.

"And it is pretty. He obviously has good taste."

Well! At least she was trying to make up. I explained that just at the moment Alex didn't earn very much money so he probably couldn't afford real silver. "It was sweet of him to buy me *anything*."

"Yes, it was," said Katie. She added that according to her dad, Polish workers were being exploited. "They come over here desperate for jobs and get taken advantage of. Paid peanuts. Hardly enough to live on. But they are the *best*. If you want a good job done, get a Polish worker. That's what my dad says."

She was trying really hard. I felt a surge of gratitude towards her. I said that once Alex was his own boss he could charge people whatever he liked and then he would earn proper money.

"I s'pose he'll have to wait a while, though," said Katie.

I told her, not necessarily. "It might happen quite soon."

She was curious to know more, but I wasn't letting on. There are some things you can't talk about even with your best friend. Katie has been brought up to be *so* conventional. She would be horrified if she knew what I was planning.

Beth wouldn't; she would say, go for it! But I couldn't tell Beth if I couldn't tell Katie. That wouldn't be fair.

Now that Alex had bought a present for me, I was desperate to buy one for him. I knew just the thing! But I needed to go into town, to Waterstone's. I told Katie next day that I had a history club meeting during the lunch break, and headed out of school the minute the bell rang. We are not supposed to leave school during the day, but lots of kids slip out to the local kebab shop or the fish and chip shop and get back in again without anyone noticing. Being one of the *good* girls, I'd never done it before; but suddenly I was one of the bad ones. The ones who got detentions and ignored the rules and forgot to do their homework.

I ran all the way to the underground, jumped off two stops later, ran all the way to Waterstone's, grabbed the book I wanted, paid for it, galloped back to the underground and arrived in school just in time for the start of afternoon classes.

"Why are you all hot and panting?" hissed Katie. "Where have you been?"

I said, "History club. I told you."

"There wasn't one! I checked. I asked Emily Groves and she said there aren't any more meetings until next term."

She'd been *spying* on me. My best friend... not trusting me!

"You've been into town! Why didn't you tell me?"

I wasn't quite sure why I hadn't told her. Normally I would have done. Normally we tell each other everything.

"What have you got? Have you been buying books?" She grabbed at my Waterstone's bag before I could stop her. "*Teach Yourself Spanish*... what d'you want that for?"

"It's not for me."

"So who's it – " She stopped. "*Him?* Why's he want to learn Spanish? He can't even speak English properly!"

I snatched the book away from her and put it back in its bag. "Never know when it might come in useful," I said. And what business was it of hers anyway? Why did everyone have to keep *interfering in my life?*

"You could have told me," muttered Katie.

Later that evening, when everyone else was downstairs, I shut myself in my room and wrote a message – *To Alex, with Love and Kisses from Tamsin.* Then I put the book in a Jiffy bag which I'd begged from Katie's mum, with a first-class stamp which I'd also begged. If I posted it tomorrow, it would reach him on Thursday – the day that me and Ellie were being shunted off to the Aunties.

I was tempted to sneak away after school and give it to him in person, but Katie was being such a grouch that I was scared she'd shop me to her mum. I didn't want Katie's mum being upset with me. She's a bit what Dad calls *strait-laced*, but I do actually admire her. She gives me books to read. The sort of stuff I might probably never think to pick up, if it weren't for her. *Jane Eyre*, for instance, and *Pride and Prejudice*. Oh, and *A Tale of Two Cities*, which I really enjoyed because of it being about history. She knew I'd like that one! She told me after that to try *Barnaby Rudge*, which is also about history. I haven't got around to it yet, but it's on my list, along with the rest of Dickens. Sometimes I think I might actually became a teacher one day, and that would be thanks to Katie's mum. I really wouldn't like her to think badly of me.

Fortunately, not even Katie could stop Alex and me. We texted every night, at bedtime; not just once, but over and over. Because I was staying for three days Katie's mum had put me in the spare room, where I could be private.

"I suppose you're *phoning* him," said Katie.

I told her that that was where she was wrong: texting is not the same as phoning. We had actually tried speaking on the phone, but it was quite frustrating. There's not a great deal that you can talk about when you don't properly understand each other's language. But we could manage just fine without talking! When you are in love, you don't need words; that is what is so wonderful about it.

School broke up on Friday, but me and Ellie had to leave town on Thursday cos the friend she was staying with was flying off to Portugal the following day. That was what other people did: they flew off to places. Me and Ellie just got bundled on to the train at Liverpool Street to go to *Clacton*.

Ellie said, "I like Clacton!"

I looked at her with distaste. "Since when?"

"I've always liked it. It's just as nice as Portugal."

I said, "How do you know? You've never been to Portugal. You've practically never been anywhere. We never go anywhere!"

"We're going to Florida at Christmas," said Ellie. "Dad's promised. You're only in a hump cos they won't let you see your boyfriend."

I said, "So would you be!"

"No, I wouldn't! I wouldn't care. I haven't got a boyfriend."

I said, "*Oh?* What happened to Obi?"

"He's not my boyfriend any more."

"Why? Has he ditched you?"

"No, I just grew out of him. Mum says you'll grow out of yours. She says it's just a passing phase. She told Dad not to get so steamed up cos by the end of the summer you'll have come to your senses."

What did Mum know about anything? People like her and Ellie are just fickle. I'd heard about Mum and all the boyfriends she'd had when she was young. She actually laughed about it. She thought it was *funny*. I didn't think it was funny. I thought it just went to show how shallow Mum's emotions were. She had obviously never been truly genuinely in love. If she had, she wouldn't be talking about passing phases and telling Dad that I would come to my senses.

I was about to relay to Ellie – whose emotions, I reckoned, were every bit as shallow as Mum's – when my phone started warbling.

"Who's that?" said Ellie.

"Excuse me," I said, "but it's none of your business."

"Is it your boyfriend?"

I turned away from her, shielding the screen with one hand.

"Is it a text? You're not supposed to be texting! What does it say?"

Like I was going to tell *her*?

"*Tee queero?*" She'd bounced across the seat and was peering over my shoulder. "What's that mean?"

"Nothing to do with you. Go away! It's private."

"You're not supposed to be private! Dad s – "

"Buzz off!" I jabbed my elbow hard into her ribs and she fell back, with a squawk.

"That hurt!"

"Good."

"You could have broken something!"

"Serve you right if I had. Are you actually being *paid* to spy on me?"

"I'm not spying, but you shouldn't be talking to him!" She rubbed her ribs. "I could tell Mum."

"So tell her," I said.

"I could!"

"Go ahead. Think I care?"

"I won't," said Ellie, "if you tell me what *tee queero* means."

Te quiero… I love you. He'd already made a start on learning Spanish!

"D'you want to see his photo?" I said.

"I know what he looks like!"

I showed her anyway. She said, "Yeah, cool."

"You'd know he wasn't English," I said, "wouldn't you? He looks sort of… mysterious. Don't you think?"

It felt a bit degrading, asking Ellie, of all people! But I just couldn't seem to stop myself.

She said, "I dunno. Maybe. I never thought about it. Is that Polish he wrote you?"

"No," I said, "it's Spanish."

"So why won't you tell me what it means? I suppose it's all *lovey dovey*. Yuck yuck!"

I said, "Wouldn't you like to know?"

"*Just tell me what it means!*"

I felt my lips curve themselves into this big dreamy smile. I wanted to say something cold and cutting that would put her in her place, but I had these great bubbles of happiness frothing and foaming inside me.

"It means that Mum is wrong," I said. "We're never going to stop loving each other!"

CHAPTER NINE

The Aunties were waiting at the station to meet us. Auntie Mo and Auntie May. They are in fact *Mum's* aunties, which makes them our great aunts, but great aunt is far too much of a mouthful. They have always just been the Aunties.

I think they're both a bit eccentric; at least, that's what

Dad says. Auntie May is the senior Auntie, the one who makes all the decisions. She is really bossy, which is probably because she used to be head teacher at a primary school. She's tall and skinny and likes to wear purple. Auntie Mo is smaller and softer, like a squidgy bun. She mostly does what Auntie May tells her to do. They have lived in the same house in Clacton all their lives, and Auntie Mo has hardly ever been out of it as she was the one who stayed at home to look after her dad. That is, Mum's *grandad*. A strange thought! Anyway, Auntie Mo used to give piano lessons to little kids, and sometimes still does, but she has never actually had a job in the real world. She is very innocent. She's never been married, and neither has Auntie May. I'm not even sure they've even had boyfriends. They're a bit weird, if you ask me.

Auntie Mo prattled happily like she always does as Auntie May drove us home. "So glad your mum and dad are working. So lovely for them! Must be such a worry, I always think. Such an *insecure* profession."

"They can't help it!" cried Ellie. "They're like me...

I am *born* to be an actor. It's the same for Mum and Dad!"

"But such a high price," sighed Auntie Mo. "Never knowing when your next job is coming along. And all those months out of work!"

"*Resting*," said Ellie. "But the big break could come at any moment! This movie Dad's doing… this could be his chance!"

I said, "Yeah, yeah, yeah!" Not that anybody took any notice. Auntie May was busy driving (she never talks when she drives) and Auntie Mo is far too easily impressed. Well, I think she is. Ellie doesn't need any encouragement; it is all fantasy! By the time we arrived in Grange Road, she already had Dad in Hollywood, with his name up in lights.

"It could happen," she said earnestly. "All you need is one big break!" And then she looked at me and pulled a face and said, "She's just in a mood cos of not being allowed to see her boyfriend."

"Yes, we've heard about that," said Auntie May. "He doesn't sound very *suitable*, Tamsin, dear."

"He's Polish," said Ellie.

"I know, my dear; your mum said. And quite old, I believe. Never mind!" Auntie May patted my hand. "You're still very young, you'll get over it. No broken hearts at your age!"

"That's what Father said," said Auntie Mo. "And look what happened there."

There was a split second of freezing silence.

"I don't think," said Auntie May, "that we need to bring that up, do we?"

She said it quite gently, but sometimes I have noticed that when Auntie May's seeming to be gentle it's actually like an iron fist in a velvet glove kind of thing.

Auntie Mo immediately grew flustered and said, "Oh, well, no, of course not!" and went scuttling off indoors. If I hadn't been in such a sulk I'd have wanted to know more, but Ellie had already started burbling again about Dad becoming a big star and the moment passed. Still sulking, I followed Auntie Mo, into the house.

The Aunties' house is very old; Victorian, I think. It is

tall and narrow, and has been divided into two, with the back part cut off from the front, except for the kitchen, which is down in the basement. The back part is let out into rooms, mostly to little old ladies who have lived there for ever. The Aunties prefer little old ladies because old ladies are not troublesome like young people. They're quiet and well-behaved and don't play loud music all the time or have noisy parties with everyone getting drunk and being sick. Kind of boring, really, but I suppose you can understand it.

As a result of all the little old ladies, me and Ellie had to share a bedroom. More than just *kind of* boring: totally, completely, and *utterly* boring. I needed my own space! How could I daydream with Ellie lying there? *Watching me. Listening. Talking.* I needed to be by myself!

Six weeks had never loomed so long. When we were little I used to enjoy staying with the Aunties. Apart from anything else, there was the sheer *unusualness* of being at the seaside. Donkey rides and crazy golf and building castles in the sand. Walking along the front, stuffing ourselves with candy floss. Dodgem cars and slot machines. Fish and chip suppers, and going off for picnics with the kids next door.

But that was *then*; this was *now*. I was too old for all that stuff. How dare Auntie May try to belittle my emotions? Telling me I'd get over it! "No broken hearts at your age". What did she know about anything? I bet she'd never been in love in her life, withered old stick.

I'm not normally ageist as it's every bit as bad, in my opinion, as sexism or racism. I mean, people can't help being old. It's not their fault. But Auntie May makes me so mad!

And then I remembered Auntie Mo's remark. "That's what Father said… and look what happened there." Suddenly, I was really curious. *Father* was Mum's grandad. Who had he been talking about? Surely not either of the Aunties! Mum's mum? In other words, my grandmother, whom I never knew because she died when Mum was a baby. Or maybe Mum herself? Yes! That sounded more like it. Mum, with her neverending stream of boyfriends. I bet it was Mum!

I knew it wouldn't be any use asking Auntie May; she wouldn't tell me. Neither would Auntie Mo, unless I could get her on her own. It took me ages to corner her, but I managed it at last, as she was coming out of the bathroom later that night, all wrapped up in a fluffy pink dressing-gown.

I said, "Auntie Mo?"

"Yes, dear."

"You know what you said earlier, about your dad saying the same thing and look what happened?"

"What was that, dear?"

"When Auntie May was telling me how you don't get broken hearts when you're only my age." I could hear the note of bitterness creeping into my voice. "You said that's what your dad said."

"Did I, dear?" Auntie Mo clutched nervously at the neck of her dressing-gown.

"Who did he say it about?"

"Goodness me!" She gave a little trill. "I don't remember."

I knew that she did; she was just scared of Auntie May.

"Was it my mum?"

"Malorie? Oh, no, dear!" She shook her head, quite vigorously.

"*Her* mum?"

"Pam." She sighed. "Poor Pam! She died so young. Such a terrible tragedy."

"So was it her?"

"No, dear, certainly not! Pam was a good girl. She never did anything to upset Father."

"It wasn't Auntie May?" I couldn't believe it!

Auntie Mo gave a little titter. "May? The very idea! What a thing to accuse her of."

I said, "So who?" And what thing? "Auntie Mo," I said, "it wasn't you, was it?"

At that moment a door closed somewhere below and we heard footsteps along the hall. Auntie Mo said, "It's not something we really talk about dear." And then she was off, scuttling along the passage and diving into her room like a frightened rabbit. Really annoying! I love a mystery, but I wanted to get to the bottom of this one. I tried talking about it in bed with Ellie, but she wasn't interested.

"Who cares?" she said. "Whatever it was, it was centuries ago."

"Decades," I said. "*Actually*."

"Whatever." Ellie shrugged her shoulders.

"About 1950, it must have been." When Auntie Mo was young.

"Like I said", said Ellie. "Centuries."

I hate it when people are so careless about dates.

"I'm still going to keep on at Auntie Mo," I said. "I bet you it was her!"

But Auntie Mo can be very stubborn. It didn't matter how much I prodded and poked, she still wouldn't tell me. She even tried that old person's thing of saying her memory had gone. I hate it when old people do that! I know in some cases it may be true, but more often I'm sure it's just a ploy. What Auntie Mo was really saying was, "Don't ask me, I'm not allowed to talk about it."

I spent all that first weekend thinking about Alex. Texting him. Gazing at his picture. Secretly kissing it under the duvet at night. Sleeping with it beneath my pillow. Kissing it again when I woke up. When Ellie wasn't around to bother me I lay on my bed, daydreaming. I lay there for hours at a time. Auntie May said it wasn't natural; she said, "Dwelling on things never did anyone any good." Sometimes, to stop her nagging, I went out for long lonely walks along the sea front. Quite often, as I walked, I passed boys and girls with their arms round each other, and the pain of not being with Alex was so bad I was almost tempted to catch the first train back to London and tell him that I couldn't bear it any longer.

"We have to run away *now*!"

On Sunday evening, Mum rang up. "We've just done Wolverhampton," she chirped. "Next stop Newcastle!"

I knew I ought to ask her how it was going, but I just couldn't bring myself. I didn't care how it was going!

I didn't care if all the reviews were hideous and the audience non-existent. She didn't care about me; why should I care about her?

Mum said, "Tammy? Are you still there?"

I grunted into the telephone.

"Oh, darling, you're not still cross with me? Please say you're not!"

"Why should I be cross?" I said sarcastically. "I'm having a wonderful time."

Mum heaved a sigh; deep and quivering down the line. "Listen, angel, I know you think you'll never forgive me, but this isn't intended as a punishment. You were going to stay with the Aunties anyhow. Nothing's changed! All I'm asking is that you give it six weeks, and then – "

What? I could go out with Alex?

"Then we'll see how you feel. And we'll plan something really big for your birthday! How about that?"

I said, "You won't be here for my birthday."

"I'll be back the following week, and with any luck so will your dad. You be thinking what you'd like to do!"

I knew what I'd like to do. I knew what I was *going* to do. Mum wouldn't be here for my birthday and neither would I. I bounced the phone back on to its rest.

"You never asked how the play was doing." Ellie looked at me accusingly. "You never asked her anything!"

I said, "No, I left that to you."

"You should have asked as well!"

"Chill your beans," I said.

"Chill yours!" retorted Ellie.

"Girls, girls, that is enough," said Auntie May. "But I do think," she added, looking rather hard at me, "that you might have been a bit kinder to your mother."

Kind? Why should I be kind to Mum? She was ruining my life! Except that she wasn't, cos I wasn't going to let her. My mind was made up: in five weeks and two days' time, Alex and I would be together, and nothing would ever part us again.

"Where are you off to now?" said Auntie May.

Sullenly I said, "I'm going up to my room."

"You spend far too much time in your room. It's not healthy."

I said, "Now I can't even go to my *room*? What's the problem? D'you think I've got a man up there, or something?"

Ellie giggled. Auntie Mo gasped and clapped a hand to her mouth. Auntie May just shook her head.

"I'm going to *read a book*," I said. "If that's all right?"

Slamming the door behind me, I headed up the stairs. And that was when I saw her: the strange girl on the landing...

CHAPTER TEN

The reason she was strange was that she didn't say anything; just stood there, staring. Not even staring, really. More like… vacant. Like in some kind of a trance. It gave me a bit of a shock, as people from the back of the house are not meant to come through into the front part. The front part is private. There is a door at the top of the basement stairs, but it's supposed to be kept locked. Obviously *someone* must have forgotten. Not me! I never use it. Me and Ellie aren't allowed in what Auntie May refers to as "the guests' quarters". In any case, just because the door wasn't locked didn't give this total stranger the right to come wandering through.

What with one thing and another I wasn't feeling particularly friendly, but you can hardly just push past people without saying anything. Especially when they are *trespassing*. So I said "hello?", expecting she would at least explain what she was doing there, but it was like she never even heard me; or if she did she wasn't taking any notice.

"Are you looking for someone?" I said.

Her eyes slid vaguely in my direction, but she still didn't say anything.

"I mean, in case you hadn't realised – " you have to give people the benefit of the doubt, she mightn't be quite all there – "you're not really supposed to be in this part of the house."

The eyes swam away again and she stared off into space, with this far-away look and a slight frown on her forehead. Maybe she was on drugs; they could frazzle your brain. She didn't actually look dangerous, but the fact was she had *no right* to be there. Bad enough the house being full of old ladies using up all the rooms and me and Ellie having to share, without one of their granddaughters, or whoever she was, wandering all about the place.

Well, if she wasn't going to *talk*. I turned and went back downstairs. Auntie May said, "Why, here's madam come back! Does she intend to apologise?"

"Sorry," I said, "I didn't mean to be rude. Actually I just came to tell you that there's a strange girl out there."

Auntie May's eyebrows shot up into her hairline. "What kind of strange girl?"

"I don't know. She's just standing there."

We all trooped out into the hall, Auntie May in the lead. At the last minute, Ellie skipped ahead. Her voice came shrieking back: "I can't see anyone!"

I pushed past Auntie Mo, who was dithering. The upstairs landing was empty; the girl had disappeared.

"She was up there." I pointed.

Ellie scampered up the stairs and along the passage. "She's not here now!"

"Try the rooms," quavered Auntie Mo.

Ellie did so, and reported them all clear.

"She must have gone back down," I said. "I told her she shouldn't be here."

Auntie May, looking grim, headed off in the direction of the basement. I noticed that Auntie Mo was shaking.

"It's all right," I said. "It was only a girl. She wasn't actually doing anything."

But it wasn't the girl that was making Auntie Mo shake, it was the fear that she might have been the one to have left the basement door unlocked.

"I do it, you know... I forget! May gets so cross with me."

I sometimes feel sorry for poor Auntie Mo. She is so meek and gets so easily flustered. And Auntie May is *such* a tyrant. I would have hated to be at her primary school when she was head teacher.

Fortunately she came back up to say that the door at the top of the basement stairs was both locked and bolted, just as it ought to be, so that was a relief. Auntie Mo stopped shaking. But then Ellie cried out that the front door had the chain on – "She couldn't have got out that way!" – and Auntie Mo went into a quiver all over again because that meant the intruder was still somewhere in the house, probably hiding under one of the beds or in a cupboard.

"And why would she be doing that?" said Auntie May.

"Well, you know… if she was a burglar," pleaded Auntie Mo.

"Tamsin, did she look like a burglar?"

"I don't know," I said. "I don't know what burglars look like. She didn't have a swag bag." Auntie May breathed in, rather deeply. "Sorry," I said, "sorry! But I mean she didn't have any tools or anything. She looked more like maybe she was on drugs, or something? Kind of… out of it. You know?" I demonstrated how she'd stood there, with this glassy expression. Auntie May made a loud tutting noise.

"Are you sure you're not making this up?"

"I'm not," I said. "I saw her!"

To keep Auntie Mo happy I went with Ellie and peered into every cupboard and under every bed, but there wasn't a sign of the strange staring girl. Auntie Mo begged Auntie May to call the police, but Auntie May wouldn't hear of it.

"Make ourselves look complete fools! How, pray, was this creature supposed to have gained entry?"

It was a puzzle. All the doors were locked, and the windows, too. Auntie May said that either I had an overactive imagination or it had been my misguided idea of a joke.

"In which case," she said, "I am not amused."

I protested, in vain, that it wasn't a joke. "I saw her! I spoke to her!"

"And did you by any chance get a reply?"

Reluctantly I was forced to admit that I hadn't. But I am not the sort of person to imagine things. Mum always says I am the straightforward, level-headed one of the family – or was, until I fell in love with Alex. That was something she'd never expected! I hadn't expected it, either, to tell the truth. Maybe Auntie May was right, and my mind was starting to play tricks. But I *knew* I had seen the girl!

"Perhaps it was a ghost," said Ellie.

Auntie Mo gave a little whimper. Auntie May, drawing herself up very straight and stiff, coldly informed Ellie that "We have never had ghosts in this house and we do not intend to start now. Kindly don't talk nonsense. I suggest we all forget about it."

Later, in bed, Ellie said, "I bet it *was* a ghost."

I certainly preferred the idea of a ghost to the thought that my mind might be playing tricks. "But whose could it have been?"

"Someone who died a horrible death and they've come back to haunt."

"But why haunt me?"

"Cos you're in a state," said Ellie. "You're all lovesick and swooning. That's when they get at people."

It made a sort of sense. And the house *was* old. But the ghost hadn't been!

"She looked modern," I said.

"Some ghosts are," said Ellie. "Don't always have to be from history. What was she wearing?"

I closed my eyes, trying to conjure up the memory.

"Jeans?" said Ellie, trying to be helpful. "T-shirt? Jacket?"

"A dress," I said. "A blue dress."

"Like from now? Or olden times?"

"Not olden times." But not from now, either. "Sort of... old-fashioned. But not very. Not like Victorian, or anything. More like... when Mum was young, maybe?"

"Can't you *describe* it?"

"I didn't really notice."

"God, you're so useless!" said Ellie. "You'd never make an actress. You never notice anything!"

"She had dark hair," I said.

"What sort of style?"

"Sort of… curled."

"Like it had been *permed*?"

"Could be."

"Hm… " Ellie sat cross-legged, hugging her knees to her chest. "I know, I know!" She rocked, triumphantly. "I know who it could have been!"

"Who?"

"Mum's mum! *She* died a horrible death."

"She died having a baby," I said.

"You saying that's not horrible?"

"She died in *hospital*."

"She could still come back and haunt us!"

"Ye-e-es… but this girl was younger. She only looked like my age."

"But you said she had dark hair," urged Ellie. "Mum's mum had dark hair. Like Mum has dark hair. I've got dark hair!"

And I was mousy blonde, like my dad. But I shook my

head. I'd seen pictures of our grandmother; I knew what she looked like.

"There was a *sort* of resemblance," I said. "but it definitely wasn't her."

"Got to be someone!!" Ellie rocked again; she was enjoying herself. "Who else could it be?"

"I don't know. Maybe I was just imagining it." I was almost beginning to think that I must have done. "Whatever you do," I said, "don't go bothering the Aunties, cos Auntie Mo will freak and Auntie May will get all frozen, you know like she does. She's already mad at me, I don't want her getting any madder."

Ellie sighed. "OK, but if she appears again you've got to promise to tell me."

The days went grinding on. Five-and-a-half weeks to my birthday… five weeks to my birthday. Thirty-five days. Thirty-four days. Thirty-three, thirty-two, thirty-one… I marked them off, secretly, in a notebook. It was very difficult doing anything secretly with Ellie around. The kids next door had gone away, and she always seemed to be at my elbow, whining about having nothing to do, demanding to know what *I* was doing.

"What are you up to? What are you writing? Are you writing to him? You're not supposed to be writing to him! You're not supposed to be in touch with him *at all*. What have you got in your notebook?"

Like it was any of her business. I told her to go away and get a life and let me get on with mine, but when Ellie is bored she clings like a limpet. I sometimes think she has no inner resources at all. I asked Auntie May one day if I could borrow her library card, and Ellie immediately shrieked, "What d'you want to go to the library for?"

I said, "A book, would you believe?"

"I want a book, too!" said Ellie. "I'll come with you."

There wasn't any shaking her. She *insisted*. Auntie May said, "Well, for goodness' sake, don't discourage her!"

"That's right," said Ellie. "You're not the only person who reads! *I've* done the whole of *Harry Potter*."

And I was doing the whole of *Nicholas Nickleby*, which

was going to take me for ever. Katie's mum had lent it to me for the holiday. I didn't need another *reading* book. What I wanted was a book about Spain. I wanted to fix on a good place for me and Alex to go. Somewhere warm and sunny, where we could swim and lie on the beach...

Normally I'd have searched on the web, but the Aunties don't have a computer. Auntie May doesn't like them, and Auntie Mo says she doesn't understand them. It's like being on a desert island, cut off from normal civilisation. I'd been promised a laptop for my birthday, but that was still four weeks away. Twenty-eight days, twenty-seven days, twenty-six, twenty-five...

Oh, God! I couldn't wait another twenty-five days. I had to speak to Alex *now*. Right away. I needed to hear his voice, to reassure myself. To know that he still loved me...

I forced myself to wait until both Ellie and Auntie May were out of the house and Auntie Mo was giving a piano lesson, then dialled his number. *Please let him answer! Please let his phone be switched on!* And then he was there, at the other end of the line, and I felt this great sense of relief.

"Alex, it's me!"

"Tamsin?"

"Where are you?"

"I at work. Where you?"

"In Clacton. In my bedroom."

"Is all right we speak?"

"No, but I don't care! I had to. I miss you *so much!*"

"I miss you, Tamsin!"

"It's still another three whole weeks before we can be together. I don't think I can bear it!"

"Three week a long time."

"That's why I had to ring. I thought you might forget who I am."

"This a joke, yes?"

"Yes!" I giggled, a bit hysterically. "I'm crossing off the days!"

"We still go Spain?"

 169

"It's the only way we can be together! If – " I faltered slightly – "if you still want us to be together?"

He said, "This another joke?"

"I'm serious! They're just going to keep saying I'm too young, you're too old, I'm not allowed to see you, I – "

"OK," said Alex. "Chill!" And then he laughed and said, "I learn good English, no?"

"What about your Spanish?"

"Si, si! Español. You teach me when we there."

So that was it! We were going. I switched off the phone and curled myself up in the duvet to dream. Me and Alex, on a sandy beach... wrapped together, with the sun beating down, the waves lapping as we kissed... and kissed... and went on kissing... and no one to stop us. No one to interfere. Just him and me...and the sun and the sand...

I was brought violently back to reality by Ellie crashing into the room. Since it was her room as well as mine, she no longer bothered knocking. Just barged straight in.

"What are you doing?" she squealed. "It's the middle of the day!"

I sat up crossly. "I thought you were out."

"We came back. What are you *doing*?"

"I'm not doing anything! I'm trying to relax. It's supposed to be a holiday."

"It's boring," said Ellie. She bounced herself down on to the bed. *My* bed. "Have you seen the ghost again?"

I said, "No, I haven't." Actually, that wasn't strictly true. Just occasionally, at odd moments, just now and again, I'd had the strangest feeling that I was being watched. That there was something there. Some kind of… presence. But then when I turned to look – nothing! Except just a glimpse. Just a shadow. Not scary, but a bit disturbing.

I didn't want to talk about it. I didn't even want to think about it. I hauled at the duvet. "Get your shoes off the bed!"

"They're clean," said Ellie.

"I don't care. Get them off! And just shut up about ghosts."

"Why? They're nothing to be scared of." Said Ellie.

"I said, *shut up*! I'm not scared of them."

"Then why – "

"Did you hear me?" I snatched up my pillow and hurled it at her. "If you can't shut up, just go away and leave me in peace!"

CHAPTER ELEVEN

It was one of those rare evenings when we were alone with Auntie Mo. Auntie May had gone off to a meeting of the local residents' association. According to Auntie Mo, she was "very *big*" in the association. Ellie and I exchanged glances and tried not to giggle.

"I bet she bosses them about," I said. "Like she bosses everyone."

Auntie Mo said, "She can't help it, dear. It's just her way. It's what comes of being the oldest."

"Tamsin's the oldest," said Ellie. "She bosses me all the time."

"Well, if I do," I said, "it's because you ask for it. And I don't think you should be watching any more TV," I added. "You've been sitting there in front of it all day."

Ellie turned to Auntie Mo. "You see what I mean?"

"I'm not taking sides," said Auntie Mo. "I had enough of taking sides when I was young. It always had to be me and May against the other t – " She stopped. "Against your grandmother."

She seemed suddenly flustered. I wondered what it was she had been going to say. I felt, strangely, that I ought to know – that I *did* know – but it was just a faint niggle somewhere on the far edge of my brain, and I dismissed it.

"So I can watch TV if I want", said Ellie. "Right?" She glared at me.

"If she watches TV," I said, "I'm going upstairs."

"Yes, and I know what for! You're going to speak to *him*. You think I don't know what you do up there! They text each other," said Ellie. "All the time!"

"It's more intelligent than watching TV," I said.

"But you're not supposed to be doing it!"

"And you're not supposed to sit there goggling all day! Mum wouldn't let you, if she was here."

"If Mum was here," said Ellie, "you wouldn't be talking to *him*."

"Elinor and Tamsin, please!" said Auntie Mo. "It gives me quite a headache when you start on at each other. Sisters should be *friends*. Now let's think how to pass the time agreeably, the three of us together. What would you like to do?"

Ellie opened her mouth. I knew she was going to say, "Watch TV." I jumped in over the top of her. "Let's look at photos!"

"*Again?*" said Ellie.

"I like looking at them. It's history."

"But we do it every time! We've seen them all."

"So we can see them again. It doesn't stop them being interesting."

I wasn't sure why I'd suggested it, since Ellie was quite right. We'd been looking through the family photograph albums every year for so long we knew them off by heart. But that faint niggle was still there, at the back of my mind, and it seemed to have something to do with photographs.

"What are all these loose ones?" I said. I'd pulled open the drawer where the albums were kept. "All these in this bag?" An ordinary plastic bag from Tesco, stuffed full of photographs. "I don't remember these ones! Are they some we haven't seen?"

"I don't know, dear." Auntie Mo sounded vague, as usual. "They're just the ones we've never got around to sorting. You can look at them, if you like."

I tumbled them out on to the table. Ellie immediately started scrabbling through, very fast, going, "Seen that one! Seen that one! That one's Mum, when she was a baby. That's Mum when she was at school. That's *her* mum. That's – " She stopped. "Dunno who that is."

I peered across. She was holding a photograph of four girls. It was similar to one we'd seen many times – except that in the one we'd seen there were only three girls. Auntie May, Auntie Mo, and our grandmother, who had died. And then suddenly it was as if a pop-up had appeared in my head, and I knew why Auntie Mo's remark had niggled at me. "It always had to be me and May against the other t – " *The other two*, she had been going to say. I remembered, now. Mum had once told me, ages and ages ago, that there had been four sisters. May, Maureen, Pam, and –

"Patty!"

Auntie Mo jumped. She held out a hand, slightly unsteady. "May I see?"

"Who's Patty?" said Ellie.

"She was a sister," I said.

"So why haven't I heard of her?"

"I don't know." I'd been too young, when Mum told

★ 177 ☆

me, to show any curiosity. Ancient people from long ago don't really hold much interest when you're only about six years old.

"Auntie Mo?" We both turned, to look at her. Waiting for an answer. Auntie Mo was staring fixedly at the photo. It was like she hadn't seen it for decades, which maybe she hadn't.

"I thought they'd all been got rid of," she said.

Me and Ellie flickered our eyes at each other.

"Did something horrible happen to her?" said Ellie. "She didn't *die*, did she?"

"In a manner of speaking," said Auntie Mo. She gave a quivering sigh. "Poor Patty! Father told us never to mention her name in front of him. And so, of course, we didn't. We always obeyed Father. All of us, except Patty."

"What did she do?" I said.

"Oh, my dear! It was very shocking, at the time. You have to understand, things were different in those days. It was the 1950s: '51, '52… Patty was sixteen. The baby of the family." Auntie Mo smiled, as if at fond memories. "So pretty she was. And clever with it. She got a scholarship, you know. Father was so proud of her! She was always his favourite. His little Patty."

Auntie Mo smiled again, lost somewhere in her memories. Ellie and I waited, not quite patiently. Ellie was almost jigging up and down on her seat, desperate for Auntie Mo to go on. To hear the story.

"I shouldn't really be telling you this." Auntie Mo cast a nervous glance towards the door.

"It's all right," I said. "Auntie May won't be back for ages."

"And we promise not to tell on you," said Ellie.

"But we ought to know, cos after all, it is family."

"And it can't have been *that* bad," said Ellie. "Not unless she had a boyfriend who cheated on her and she murdered him and is rotting in jail."

I said, "*Ellie.*" And then I thought, maybe she had a boyfriend and got pregnant and they took the baby away and put her in a lunatic asylum. They used to do that, way back then. I'd read about it. Unlike

Ellie, however, I was discreet enough not to say so.

"*Pleeeze*," begged Ellie. "Now we've seen her photo…
please tell us!"

"Well, I suppose you're old enough," said Auntie Mo.

I thought, lunatic asylum…

"It was a man, wasn't it?" said Ellie. "I bet it was a man!"

"Yes, my dear, I'm afraid it was. A most unsuitable
man! Frank, I remember his name was. Frank Bagley. That
was it. Oh, he was a handsome devil! I'll give him that."

Ellie sniggered. I said, "How was he unsuitable?"

"Oh, in every way. He was far too old, for one thing.
She was only sixteen, still a schoolgirl. He must have been
thirty, if he was a day."

Ellie shot a meaningful glance in my direction.
I ignored it.

"What was he doing in Clacton?" I said.

"He was a mechanic," said Auntie Mo. "In a *garage*."
She said it in hushed tones, like we were supposed to be
shocked. Ellie shot another glance at me. I kicked her,
harder than before.

"Our family had always been professionals! Father was an accountant. Very highly thought of. And Patty… she was going to go to university. It was quite something, in those days. Not many people did. 'Specially girls."

"So what happened?" said Ellie.

"Well, naturally, Father put his foot down. Said she wasn't to see him any more."

"But she did." Hint, hint. Ellie jabbed at me with a finger. I felt like punching her.

Auntie Mo sighed. "She was always very headstrong. Between you and me, she was rather spoilt, what with being Father's favourite."

Well, at least Ellie couldn't accuse *me* of being spoilt. I wasn't anyone's favourite.

"Did he find out?" said Ellie.

"Not until it was too late." Aunt Mo shook her head. "She was a sly one! She kept her secrets. Even from her own sisters! Then one day – that was it. She just took off."

I leaned forward, trying not to seem too eager. *"With him?"*

"The mechanic," said Ellie.

"*Frank,*" I said. "Did they go off together?"

"She left a note saying they were going to get married. It broke Father's heart. Mother's too, of course. But poor Father, he never got over it."

"*Did* they get married?" The question came out a bit more urgently than I'd meant it to.

"Apparently they did," said Auntie Mo. "They seemed quite happy. We had a Christmas card, years later, from New Zealand, of all places. Signed *Frank and Patty*. They had two children, as I recall… a son and a daughter."

I jabbed triumphantly, at Ellie.

"Of course – " Auntie Mo gazed sadly at the photo. "It was all too late by then. Mother was dead, and Father had had his first stroke. We tried to tell him, but we were never quite sure that he understood."

"But you wrote back?" said Ellie.

"We couldn't, you see… there was no address. We had a few more cards, and then – nothing. It must be a good ten years since we last heard. Poor Father!

He went to his grave without ever seeing his grandchildren."

I thought to myself that it was entirely his own fault. If he had only been a bit more sympathetic to the nature of true love there would have been no need for Patty to run away. He brought it on himself! But I didn't say so as I didn't want to upset Auntie Mo. Auntie Mo had sided with her dad; they probably all had. I pictured Patty, desperate, with no one to turn to. She would have loved Frank as much as I loved Alex, so I knew how she must have felt. I did think it was a pity he had to be called anything as unromantic as Frank Bagley, but on the other hand he was obviously pretty gorgeous. I stifled a giggle, and wondered if Auntie Mo would think Alex was a "handsome devil". I wished I could show her his photo! Unlike me, Alex was *definitely* photogenic.

There were a million more questions I would have liked to ask Auntie Mo. I was dying to find out everything I could about Frank and Patty! But too late. Auntie May had come blustering back from her meeting and Auntie Mo, instantly in a flutter, had gathered up the photographs and guiltily stuffed them back in the drawer. Auntie May fortunately didn't notice. She was too busy telling us about the meeting, and how she had to put "certain people" in their place.

"That Henson woman from Number 4… she has a mouth on her! And the new couple, those Beechams… only been here five minutes and think they can take over!"

We all had to sit and listen; not even Ellie dares interrupt when Auntie May is in full flow. I did try nudging at Ellie and mouthing "See?" Things *could* work out! I suppose, really and truly, I just wanted the satisfaction of saying *I told you so*. It was a relief when it finally got to be ten o'clock. Ten o'clock is the Aunties' bedtime, which means that me and Ellie also have to go upstairs. For some reason they don't like us staying down by ourselves.

As soon as we reached our room, I burst out with it: "You see? It all worked out."

"How d'you know?" said Ellie. "You're only saying it cos it's what you'd like to believe."

"Pardon me? Didn't she get married and have kids?"

"So what? Doesn't necessarily mean it worked out. Might just mean she got stuck."

I said, *"Stuck?"*

"Like, you know… with kids." Ellie looked at me slyly. "Hope you don't," she said.

I flushed angry and embarrassed. "You want to go and wash your mouth out!"

"Why? It's not rude. You don't have to get all twisted."

"You have absolutely *no right* to say something like that."

"Like what?"

"You know like what!"

"Well it wasn't me, anyway," said Ellie, "it was Dad."

"Dad?" I stared at her, appalled.

"I heard him talking about it with Mum. He said

you weren't very streetwise and you'd be easy to take advantage of. 'Specially by someone so much older."

I denied it, indignantly. "Alex wouldn't *ever* – I choked – "*ever* take advantage! What did Mum say?"

Ellie screwed up her face. "Can't remember. Don't think I heard. Mum just says not to make too much fuss cos she reckons you'll get over it. It's just a passing phase."

"Didn't stop her sending me to bloody Clacton! The twenty-first century," I said, bitterly, "and they're still behaving like it's back in the Dark Ages."

Frank and Patty, all over again. History repeating itself! But that's what history so often does. Except that there wasn't any excuse for Mum and Dad; they were actors, not boring repressed accountants. Actors are supposed to be broad-minded, liberal sort of people. They were treating me like I had committed some kind of sin. Like *Alex* had committed some kind of sin. I hated them for that. It was so unfair! Alex was a truly sweet person who just wanted to love me and take care of me. Why couldn't Mum and Dad see that? Because they had never even tried, that was why. They were behaving exactly the same as Maggie's father had, and when I disappeared from their lives they would have only themselves to blame.

"Where are you off to?" said Ellie, as I marched to the door.

I said, "I am going to the *bathroom*, if that's OK with you."

"Why are you taking your phone with you?"

God, did her beady eyes miss nothing? "Might wanna call 999 and have them come and pick you up!" I said.

"Are you going to ring *him*?"

"None of your business!"

She was right, of course; I had been going to call Alex. I was going to sneak back downstairs and shut myself away in the kitchen. But I never even got as far as the top of the stairs, because there on the landing, right where she had been before, was the ghost girl. And this time, I recognised who she was…

CHAPTER TWELVE

"*Patty?*" Ellie shot up the bed, hugging her knees and staring at me, bright-eyed. "Are you sure?"

"I'm positive! She looked exactly like she did in the photo."

"I want to see!" Ellie scrambled off the bed and scurried on elaborate tip toe to the door. "Got to be *very quiet*," she whispered. "Don't want to scare her."

I hadn't thought you *could* scare ghosts, but being quiet seemed only sensible. The last thing we needed was for Auntie Mo to come wobbling out, or even worse, Auntie May. *We have never had ghosts in this house and we do not intend to start now.* But how could you stop them? Not even Auntie May had any power over ghosts.

Ellie had stuck her head round the door and was peering out on to the landing. "Can't see anything," she hissed.

I tiptoed across to join her. "She was over there." I pointed. "Just like last time."

"Not there now," said Ellie. She closed the door and went back to sit, cross-legged, on her bed. Solemnly she regarded me. "You know what this means?"

"What?"

"She's here for you."

I bleated, "Why me?"

"I told you! Cos you're in a state. About *him*. That's when they get to you. What I don't understand," said

Ellie, "is how it can be Patty. *She* didn't die a horrible death! She didn't die at all. She got married and went off to New Zealand. So how can she be back here, haunting?"

"I dunno. I s'pose – " I said it vaguely – "I s'pose ghosts can do whatever they like. There aren't any rules."

"Course there are! They can't just drift about from place to place."

"Why can't they? They're *spirits*." If they existed at all. "They can go anywhere."

Ellie looked at me, pityingly, "Shows how much you know."

"So what makes you an expert all of a sudden?"

"I've read things," said Ellie.

"What, like *Rules for Haunting*? How can you have rules for something that mightn't even exist?"

"Ghosts do exist! It's a known fact."

I clicked my tongue impatiently.

"All right," said Ellie, "what's your explanation?"

I had to admit I didn't have one.

"I'll tell you what I think," said Ellie. "*I* think you've got the wrong sister. I think it was Pam, cos she *did* die young. And she's our grandmother, so it's likely she'd hang around and haunt."

"She died in hospital," I muttered.

"Yes, but at least it was close by. Not like New Zealand. And maybe – " Ellie bounced, exultantly – "maybe she actually really died *here*, in the house… her soul died here and it was just the empty shell that went to hospital."

I squirmed uncomfortably. "Do you have to?"

"I'm just trying to make sense of it for you. If it was Pam, that means you saw a ghost. If it was Patty, it means you're going bonkers." Ellie peeled back the duvet and rolled herself into bed. "You choose!"

It took me ages to get to sleep. I kept opening my eyes and imagining that I could see ghostly figures in the moonlight. *Three times* I pretended that I needed the bathroom, just to give myself an excuse for checking out the landing. I refused to believe I was going bonkers! But I knew that it was Patty I had seen, not

Pam. Our grandmother was quite a short plump person with a dimpled face; in the photograph, Patty was already a whole lot taller. And Patty was lean and angular, more like Auntie May, and had these deep-set eyes like pools of black ink.

The eyes of the ghost girl had been just the same, deep and dark. The only difference was that in the photograph the eyes were alive and alert, concentrating on the camera. The eyes of the ghost girl had been... dead. All the light gone from them. Surely, if it was my mind playing tricks, I would have seen her exactly the same as in the photograph? And anyway, how about that first time? I hadn't even *seen* the photograph then!

As we went down to breakfast next morning Ellie paused on the landing and hissed, "Is this where she was? Where I'm standing?" I nodded. Ellie closed her eyes and let her arms drift slowly upwards.

I said, "What are you *doing?*"

"I'm getting the vibes," said Ellie. She breathed deeply, throwing her head back and flaring her nostrils. "I can't feel anything… you try!" She grabbed at me and I shook her off.

"Leave me alone, I don't want to feel vibes!"

"But it's interesting," said Ellie.

"It's not," I said, "it's creepy. Just forget about it!"

But it wasn't the sort of thing you can forget about. Even if you are not scared of ghosts, which *I am not*, it is unnerving to keep seeing people who don't exist, specially when you are the only one. Ellie, of course, couldn't stop talking about it.

"I wonder what would happen if you tried walking straight through her? Next time you ought to try, and see what happens. If you go straight through her it'll prove she's a ghost and not just your imagination. If it's your imagination, she'll just, like, disappear, and then you'll know."

I thought, know what? That my mind was cracking up?

"It'll be a psychic experiment," said Ellie.

I looked at her with distaste. "Don't you have anything you want to go and do?" I said.

"No," said Ellie. She pouted. "Drew and Chelsea aren't there and it's still raining and I'm bored!"

"So read a book! I thought you got one out of the library?"

"I did. It's boring."

"Then go and get another one!"

"I can't, it's *raining*."

I gave up at that point. "Just go and watch TV," I said. "You might as well, you're already brain-dead, you can't do any more damage." I have *no* patience with people who keep saying they are bored.

"Where are you going?" demanded Ellie.

I snapped, "Upstairs! And I don't need you coming with me."

She opened her mouth, but before she could say it – "You're going to ring *him*!" – Auntie May had appeared.

"Elinor," she said, "if you're not doing anything – "

I fled. I wasn't going to ring Alex, as it happened, cos I knew he'd be at work, but I thought that I would text him. Just *LUV & KISSES* to show that I was thinking of him. Then I would curl up under the duvet and let my mind drift... all the way to Spain, and the sun-drenched beach where we kissed the days away...

I didn't answer my mobile when it started on its merry warble; I was too deep in my daydream. When finally, reluctantly, I swam back to reality, I found I had a text from Alex in reply to mine: *LUV U. CALL ME.* I called immediately. My heart leapt when I heard his voice telling me how he missed me and longed to be with me. A small unworthy part of my brain – I could admit it, now – had always had this fear that once I was away he would forget me. That he would find someone else; someone older, more sophisticated. Someone *prettier*. I'd seen the way pretty girls looked at him. I'd seen their eyes flicker from me to Alex and back again, trying to work out what he saw in me. He could get any girl he wanted! But he didn't want any girl: he wanted *me*.

Without even stopping to think about it, I said yes – yes, yes, *yes*! – when he begged to be allowed to come down to Clacton on Saturday.

"I need see you, Tamsin! I miss you so much!"

I said, "I miss you, too." And then it burst out of me, in a great unstoppable splurge: "I'm just so miserable without you! I can't stop thinking about you. I don't know what I'm going to do if we can't be together!"

"So is all right if I come?"

I said, "Yes! *Please*. Come!" I knew we could only snatch at the very most a couple of hours before the Aunties started asking questions, but we had been separated for *so long*. Even just a couple of hours would be precious. What was most precious of all was that Alex missed me as much as I missed him... how could I ever have doubted him?

I bounced out of my room, my heart pounding, only to be brought up short by the now familiar figure of the ghost girl standing in her usual spot, on the landing. I hesitated; she seemed to be looking straight at me. I gave a small, uncertain smile, but there was no response. Not even a flicker.

She just went on staring; that dead, glassy-eyed stare.

Suddenly panicked, I shot past and leapt down the stairs in three great bounds. When I turned at the bottom to look back, she had gone.

I found I was trembling. My knee caps were bouncing, and my limbs were all shivery. Even my teeth were like castanets. I clamped my jaws together and ran on wobbly legs down the hall. Auntie Mo was in the kitchen, filling a kettle. She beamed at me.

"Just in time!" she said. "I'm making a cup of tea. Sit down, and we'll have it together. I've got some of those biscuits you like. Cherry shortcake. Or was that your sister? Maybe it was your sister. I know it was one of you. Well, if you don't care for shortcake there's always digestive. The chocolate ones." She giggled. "I'm not supposed to eat chocolate, May says it's bad for me. But the way I see it, you have to have a bit of a treat now and again."

Auntie Mo prattled on. For once, I was grateful for her burble. I sank on to a chair and locked my kneecaps to stop them bouncing. Auntie Mo pushed biscuits at me and I ate them mechanically, without even tasting them. Auntie Mo was pleased.

"I got them specially," she whispered. "I smuggled them in without May knowing. Have as many as you like, dear! Just don't tell her."

I munched obediently. I didn't say anything about the ghost girl; it would only have thrown Aunt Mo into a fluster. I didn't intend to say anything to Ellie, either. I knew she would be cross with me. "Did you try walking through her? Did you at least try *touching* her?"

I hadn't done either of those things; I'd been too busy quaking. And now I was going to be scared stiff every time I went upstairs. I was such a coward! Ghosts can't hurt you – specially not this one. Not if it was Patty. She and I were like… soul mates. Like there was a special bond between us, linking us over the years. If we could only find some way of communicating…

It was while I was lying in bed that night, wide awake, listening to Ellie gently snoring, that it came to me. I suddenly knew what was happening. Patty was *trying* to communicate. That must be it! She was trying to tell me something. That was why she was here. She'd come because she understood how desperate I felt, being torn apart from Alex. She'd been through it herself! She wanted to reassure me: it would all come right. If I just took one big step, like she had …

I felt so much better, now that I'd worked it out. It hadn't made any sense before. Now it made total sense! I was almost tempted to wake Ellie and tell her. I even reached across and was on the point of prodding her when at the last minute I drew back. It wouldn't be sensible to tell Ellie. She had a way of keeping on, worrying at things, nudging and poking and asking questions. "What d'you mean, '*encouraging*'? Encouraging you to what?"

I was feeling so jubilant I might just have opened my mouth and come blurting out with it. "Me and Alex are going to run away together!"

I forced myself to lie down and close my eyes. Only one more day, and I would see him again. I would touch him, I would *kiss* him. Then just two more weeks and we would be off, following in the footsteps of Frank and Patty...

I almost hoped, next morning, that the ghost girl would be there waiting for me. If she had been, I would have found some way of letting her know. Surely if I concentrated my thoughts *really hard* she would be able to pick them up? But I didn't get a chance because the landing was empty. I blamed Ellie, who was jigging about, disturbing the atmosphere. It seemed to me that ghosts would like things to be peaceful. Ellie was anything *but*.

"It's raining," she wailed. "It's always raining! It's like the monsoon. I'm sick of it!"

"Never mind," I said, "you can always watch some more telly."

"I don't want to watch more telly! Mum doesn't like me watching more than two hours a day. You know she doesn't. What are *you* going to do?"

"Dunno yet," I said. "I'll think of something."

"I'm so *bored*," said Ellie.

We went down to breakfast. Auntie May insists we all eat meals together, sitting round the big table in the kitchen. She doesn't approve of what she calls "the modern habit" of everyone eating at different times, just whenever they feel like it. As we sat there, munching cereal and Ellie saying for about the hundredth time that she was bored, the telephone rang upstairs in the hall. Auntie May, in considerable annoyance, said, "Who is that at this hour?"

"Eight o'clock in the morning!" said Auntie Mo. Shock, horror! Who would have the nerve? "If it's someone looking for a room, we haven't got any."

"Well, I know *that*," said Auntie May.

She began to push her chair back, but I leapt up. "I'll go!"

"Find out who it is," said Auntie May. "Take a message. Get their telephone number. Ask what they want. Write it down!"

She obviously didn't realise that I am well-trained in

the art of answering telephones. Mum and Dad live in daily expectation of someone like Steven Spielberg ringing up, so I am very well aware of the importance of taking messages.

I picked up the phone and in my best telephone voice said, "Hello? Can I help you?"

"Well, I'm hoping so," said a voice at the other end. It was a woman's voice, with some kind of accent. Australian, maybe. "I'm looking for a Miss Munroe who used to live at this address?"

"Oh! Auntie May," I said. "Or d'you mean her sister?"

"May sounds good. May Munroe? Could I speak with her?"

"I'm afraid she's not here right at this moment," I said. "Perhaps I could take a message?"

"Yeah, sure, fine. If you could tell her that a Margaret Bagley rang? I'm just over from New Zealand, I'm in London at the moment. My telephone number – "

"Hang on a sec!" My heart was suddenly racing.

"I think I just heard the door… it might be Auntie May. Hang on, I'll go and see!"

I laid the receiver on the hall chest and went pounding back down the basement steps into the kitchen.

"It's someone called Margaret Bagley," I said.

Auntie May froze. "I am eating my breakfast just at present. I thought I told you – "

"Margaret *Bagley*?" I said. "From New *Zealand*?"

Auntie Mo gave a little excited gasp. Even Auntie May looked a bit stunned.

"I thought you might like to speak to her?"

Without a word, Auntie May swept past me and up the steps. I would have loved to follow and listen in, but it didn't seem right. We all sat there, at the breakfast table, nibbling round the edges of our toast as quietly as we could in the hope of catching the odd word. Even Ellie had stopped moaning about the rain.

"*Bagley*." She mouthed it at me. "It could be Patty's daughter!"

We waited impatiently for Auntie May to come back.

She progressed majestically down the basement steps.

She obviously wasn't intending to speak till she was settled, but you could tell, looking at her face, that she had big news.

"Well, now." She seated herself and slowly and deliberately began spreading butter on a slice of toast. "That was a Dr Bagley. Margaret Bagley. Patty's granddaughter, apparently."

"Oh!" Auntie Mo clapped a hand to her mouth.

"Her father," said Auntie May, reaching for the marmalade, "is Patty's first-born. Michael."

Auntie Mo gave a little squeak.

"Margaret, it seems, was very close to her grandmother."

Cut the toast. *Eat* the toast. God, this was killing me! I could see Auntie Mo twitching, and Ellie wriggling on her chair.

Auntie May chewed and swallowed. "She tells me she was mainly brought up by her, owing to circumstances I could not perfectly comprehend. Something to do with parental discord. The mother, so I am led to believe, departed the scene quite early on."

I clenched my fists under the table. Why for heaven's sake couldn't she just speak normal English? Ellie rolled her eyes at me.

Auntie Mo, braver than either of us, quavered, "But what of Patty?"

"Patty, I regret to report, passed away about a month ago."

A month ago! Just when we had come to Clacton. Ellie reached out with a foot and pressed it very hard on one of mine. Auntie Mo's little round face puckered. "Oh! I had so hoped – it would have been such a comfort – just to see her one last time!"

"It was entirely up to her," said Auntie May. "Had she wished to make contact, she knew where to find us. As it is, it has been left to the granddaughter. I have invited her over; she is on her way. I am suggesting she books a room at the Briarley and stays a day or two. She will doubtless be eager to make our acquaintance."

Auntie Mo was already on her feet. "We must check we have enough food! We shall have to feed her. Being from New Zealand she is bound to have a hearty appetite."

"I see no reason she should consume any more than anyone else," said Auntie May, "but obviously we must make provision. We must also do some tidying up." She looked rather pointedly at me and Ellie. "If you two girls would kindly attend to that? It is not, I think, too much to ask. The ground floor needs to be vacuumed, also dusted and polished. Quickly, quickly! She will be here before we know it."

Ellie and I snatched our last pieces of toast and crammed them into our mouths as we clattered up the basement steps. We were both bursting with things to say, and to be safely out of reach of the Aunties so that we could say them.

"This is just so *amazing*." I yanked the vacuum out of the hall cupboard and thrust it at Ellie. "Here! You vacuum, I'll dust."

For once, she didn't argue. I grabbed a duster and we rushed into the front room, shutting the door behind us.

"So she *did* die," said Ellie. "I told you ghosts had to be dead!"

"A month ago," I said. "That's when she first appeared!"

"She obviously couldn't wait to start haunting."

"But why does she look young? Every time I see her she looks *young*."

"Well..." Ellie tilted her head to one side, considering. "I guess that's cos she *was* young. When she lived here."

"But she didn't die here! She died in New Zealand."

"So?"

"How come she's haunting *here*?"

"Ghosts can haunt anywhere," said Ellie. "They can do whatever they like. There aren't any rules."

Pardon me???

"It's her *spirit*," said Ellie.

I was tempted to remind her that that was my

line, not hers; but I didn't want to quarrel with her. There was still too much to talk about.

"Know what I think?" I said. "I think our souls somehow… reached out to each other. Across the years. I think she was drawn here cos she knew what I was going through, cos it's what she went through when she was my age."

"She was sixteen," said Ellie. "You're not sixteen."

I clicked my tongue impatiently. "The point is, she was *young*. And she was *in love*. Same as I am. That's all that matters!"

"Hm." Ellie flicked the switch of the vacuum cleaner on and off, very rapidly, several times. She'd break the thing if she carried on like that. "Are you going to tell this Margaret person?" she said.

"Dunno." I'd been wondering about that. "D'you think I should?"

"S'pose it depends what she's like."

"I wonder how old she is?"

"Old," said Ellie.

"She mightn't be *that* old. Not if she's Patty's granddaughter. *We're* granddaughters."

"Mm." Ellie still sounded doubtful. "But she's a doctor."

"You can have young doctors."

"I s'pose."

We stood, thinking about it.

"I wonder if Frank's still alive?" I said.

"*He'd* be old."

"Yes, cos he was older than Patty." Like Alex was older than me. I was proud of having a mature boyfriend! I didn't want some silly spotty schoolboy. Patty had obviously felt the same way. I sighed. It was all so long ago. I didn't like to think of Frank and Patty being grey and doddery. I wanted them to stay young and in love for ever!

"I wish I could have known her," I said. I was suddenly filled with a great sadness. Sad that people grew old, sad that Patty had died before we could meet. "She's obviously been trying really hard to reach me."

"Only cos she's dead," said Ellie. "What I mean is… she didn't try and reach you while she was alive."

"That's because she didn't know about me while she was alive."

"This is it," said Ellie. "She only sensed your presence once she was dead."

We were both of us pondering what this could possibly mean when the door opened and Auntie May appeared.

"Girls," she said, "why are you not getting on with things?"

"We are," said Ellie.

"We were just going to," I said.

"Well, do so!" said Auntie May. "I want the place spotless."

CHAPTER THIRTEEN

Auntie May was in two minds whether to let me and Ellie be part of the welcoming committee or whether to banish us upstairs.

"The poor girl has come all the way from New Zealand. I should not wish to overwhelm her."

"She is bound to be feeling apprehensive," said

Auntie Mo.

"Jet lag." Auntie May spoke as one who knows. "She will need time to acclimatise."

"You mean she's just got off the plane?" I said.

"She has been here twenty-four hours. It is scarcely enough for a full recovery."

Ellie started to giggle and I had to glare at her, very hard. I wanted so much to be there to greet Patty's granddaughter! Giggling would only confirm Auntie May's belief that we'd misbehave.

"*Please*," I said. "*Please* let us be here!"

"You may be here on one condition," said Auntie May. "You do not bombard our guest with unseemly questions."

We promised to be on our best behaviour and instantly rushed upstairs to keep watch from the landing window. We had one false alarm when a middle-aged woman wheeling a suitcase appeared and seemed to be heading our way.

"Told you," hissed Ellie. "Said she'd be old!"

But the woman trundled on past, probably heading for

the bed and breakfast on the corner. Relief! I wasn't sure what I was expecting, but I desperately didn't want Patty's granddaughter to be grey and middle-aged and boring.

"Anyway," I said, "she can't be *old*, she's a granddaughter."

"She could be," said Ellie. She stood there, working things out on her fingers. "She could be *forty*!"

I wriggled uncomfortably. "Forty's not that old," I muttered. "Hey!" I suddenly grabbed Ellie's arm. "There's a cab!"

The cab drew up at the kerb and we craned our necks, trying to see who was getting out of it. A girl. Tall, with dark hair, like Patty. Carrying a backpack and wearing jeans and a T-shirt. *Young.* I just had time to say "Hah!" and give Ellie a triumphant shove before we both turned and headed for the stairs.

For the first half hour we sat meekly, side by side on the sofa like a couple of garden gnomes, speaking only when spoken to. I was bursting with questions I longed to ask, but with Auntie May's flinty eye upon me I didn't dare. She was well impressed with Patty's granddaughter, you could tell; I guess because she was what Auntie May calls *a professional person*. A doctor! Not just any old ordinary shop assistant or office worker. Auntie Mo was her normal flustery self, but Auntie May was practically bowing and scraping. It would have been quite funny if I hadn't been so eager to hear about Patty. I felt almost, by this time, as if she had been my friend. Auntie May, meanwhile, was like, "Do have a cup of coffee, do help yourself to a biscuit, you poor soul, you must be worn out!"

The girl said, "Well, not really. I'm too excited to be worn out. I never thought you'd still be living here!"

"Oh, yes," said Auntie May. "Here we were born, and here we shall die."

The girl caught my eye then, and before I could stop myself I grinned. She grinned back at me. "See, it was so strange," she said. "I knew Gran had a family somewhere over here in England, but she never actually spoke about it."

"We lost touch, sadly, many years ago."

"Yeah, I gathered. But those last couple of weeks, when she was so ill... I was with her most of the time. Towards the end she became really agitated. She kept talking about this place. This house... Ridge Mount. It was almost like she was back here, you know? But there was something that was obviously bothering her – something she seemed to feel she had to do. She kept saying, *I can't reach her, I can't get through to her!* Like it was really urgent."

I felt Ellie's finger poking me in the ribs. I edged away from her.

"It was only afterwards, going through her things, when I found an old address book with this address, that I felt I just had to come over and at least see the house, even if I couldn't locate any of the family. The first thing I did, I looked up the name Munroe in the Clacton directory, and there you were. I picked up the phone straight away. And here I am!"

"This is so exciting," said Auntie Mo. "To think that

after all these years we have Patty's granddaughter sitting here with us."

"It's pretty exciting for me, too. I was a bit scared, to tell you the truth. I reckoned there'd maybe been some kind of falling out, and even if I did make contact you wouldn't want to know me."

"My dear Margaret!" Auntie May sounded quite shocked. "We are not barbarians!"

Auntie Mo leaned forward, earnestly. "It was Patty and Father who fell out."

"Yeah... something about Gran running off with Grandpa? Not the done thing, in those days. Incidentally, call me Maggie, why not? Everyone else does. I know it's a bit clunky... Maggie Bagley." She pulled a face. "But I aim to be changing that pretty soon."

"Oh!" Auntie Mo went into fluttering mode. "You're getting married!"

At the mention of Frank I had perked up; now I felt like screaming. I wasn't interested in Maggie getting married! I wanted to hear more about Patty and her life in New Zealand. I wanted specially to hear more about her last weeks, when she had been trying so hard to get through to somebody. Who? Who was it? Was it me? And what had she been trying to say? There might be some clues, if only we could talk!

It seemed like an age before Auntie Mo finally asked one of the questions that had been burning on my lips. "And Frank? Is he – "

Maggie shook her head. "He went a few years back."

"I'm sorry to hear that," said Auntie May. "Of course, he was a great deal older than she."

"But they were happy!" The words came spluttering out of me. What did it matter if Frank was older? So long as they'd loved each other!

Ellie poked at me again, silently and secretly. Auntie May raised a frosty eyebrow. We were supposed to be on our best behaviour.

"Age isn't important." I said it defiantly. I had a right to speak! "It's being happy that matters."

"I'm sure they *were* happy," said Maggie, "to begin with.

I'm afraid I never actually knew them when they were together. They split up when my dad left home."

I stiffened, expecting Ellie to poke me again, but she just turned and studied me, in a worried kind of way. Auntie May, very briskly, said, "I cannot pretend to be surprised. Father was quite right, it was a totally unsuitable match. Nothing whatsoever in common".

"Except they loved each other!" said Ellie.

"Love!" Auntie May dismissed it scornfully. "What can you possibly know of love when you are only sixteen?"

"Was that how old she was?" Maggie sounded surprised. "I knew she and Grandpa had eloped, but I never realised she was quite so young."

"Too young. Far too young! A mere child." Auntie May didn't actually look at me as she spoke, but I knew her words were for my benefit. I felt a sort of desperation boiling up inside me.

"I think maybe the girls have built up rather a romantic picture," said Auntie Mo. She smiled fondly. "We were going through some photographs the other day and we came across one of Patty when she was – " She suddenly stopped and cast a frightened glance at Auntie May. "I had no idea it was there... I thought they had all been – "

"Removed," said Auntie May. "Quite."

Maggie said, "You removed all my gran's photos?"

"It was Father, you see." Auntie Mo sounded apologetic. "It broke his heart. He simply couldn't bear it!"

"She defied him," said Auntie May. "He was not accustomed to it. Elinor! Go and find the photo and bring it over. I daresay – " she nodded majestically in Maggie's direction – "that you would like to see it."

Ellie came back with the Tesco bag and emptied it out on to a low table. Next minute and they were all shuffling through photographs, exclaiming, explaining, *look at this, look at that! That's Father, that's Mother, that's your Great Aunt Pam.* After a bit, I couldn't restrain myself.

"Why did they split up?" I said.

Auntie May froze. "Really, Tamsin, I scarcely think

that is a proper question. What possible business can it be of yours?"

"We want to know," said Ellie. "We're interested! Did they stop loving each other?"

Slowly Maggie put down the photo she was studying. It was the one of the four girls, together. "I guess they must have done. There wasn't any bad feeling between them. I think they just… grew out of each other. Or Gran grew out of Gramps. She once told me – well, hinted – that she'd made a big mistake early on in life."

"How?" squeaked Ellie. I was glad it was Ellie who had asked the question and not me. I'm not sure I'd have been brave enough. Also, I wasn't altogether sure that I wanted to know the answer.

"She seemed to reckon she should have gone to uni and had some kind of career. I don't know if that was true, or just wishful thinking on her part?"

"Oh, it was true," said Auntie May. "It was what Father had planned. She was very gifted, academically. A real high-flyer."

"And poor old Gramps was such a sweet man! One of the sweetest men that ever lived. I loved my gran, but she wasn't the easiest. She was quite bitter towards the end."

"She knew she could have done better for herself," said Auntie May.

I squirmed crossly. Maggie frowned. "So could Gramps! He didn't deserve to be treated the way she sometimes treated him. I remember at Christmas we'd have family get-togethers and he'd come along and she'd snap at him all the time. "We'd play these games, you know?" We're a great family for games! Gran used to get so impatient. *I'm not having him on my team! I don't want him partnering me!* And he was such a dear man. Wouldn't hurt a fly!"

"Patty was always sharp-tongued," said Auntie Mo. "Of course, she was the cleverest. Though May was clever, too! She was a head teacher, you know."

The conversation swirled on, leaving me behind, stranded, like I was shipwrecked on some lonely bit of rock in the middle of nowhere. Just me on my own, with my thoughts. I'd been so sure Patty and I were soul mates! I'd felt she'd been trying to encourage me. But maybe she hadn't? *I can't reach her, I can't get through to her…* Maybe she'd been trying to warn me? *Look what happened to me, don't let it happen to you.* But it wouldn't! It couldn't! I didn't need warning. Alex and I weren't like Frank and Patty. We were in love for now and always. I would never treat Alex the way she'd treated Frank! What was the matter with people, for ever breaking up, for ever getting divorced? If you truly love someone, you don't grow out of them!

"Are you going to tell her?" said Ellie, as we did the washing-up together after lunch.

"*No.*" I shook my head, vigorously. "And you're not to, either!"

"Well, I won't if you don't want me to."

"I don't."

"All right, then, I won't." But she still couldn't drop the subject. After a pause of about a quarter of a second, she started up again. "What d'you think she was trying to say? Patty? When she said she couldn't reach you… what d'you think she wanted to say to you?"

"Dunno that she wanted to say anything to me."

"She must have wanted to say *something*."

"She was dying," I said. "When people are dying, their lives flash before them." And then it suddenly came to me. I suddenly understood! "I wasn't the one she was trying to get through to… she was trying to get through to herself! Her old self… when she was sixteen. Before she ran away." Trying to warn herself, sixty years too late… it wasn't me at all!

Ellie considered the idea, frowning, as she swished knives and forks in the sink. "I s'pose that makes sense."

"Makes perfect sense," I said.

"But you could see her. You must be psychic!"

"I s'pose I might be… just a little bit." I wondered how I felt about it. "Maybe I'm just extra-specially sensitive," I said.

Ellie wasn't too sure about that; she's supposed to be

the sensitive one. Being artistic, and everything. "You probably only saw her cos of being in love with someone Mum and Dad don't approve of, same as what she was. So long as you weren't thinking of doing what she did... which you weren't," said Ellie. "*Were* you?"

"For goodness' sake!" I snatched up a handful of knives and forks and began to dry them very rapidly and toss them into the drawer one by one, with a resounding clatter. "You're worse than the Aunties!"

The minute we had finished washing and putting away I raced upstairs to text Alex. *I LUV U I LUV U I LUV U. CU TOMORROW. XXX TAMSIN.*

On my back down, galloping as usual, for fear of what I might see, I thought I caught a glimpse of Patty, hovering silently on the landing, but I didn't turn back for a second glance. *I* wasn't the one she was trying to communicate with: *I* wasn't the one who needed warning. I'd thought we were soul mates, but we weren't. I wished she would just go away and leave me alone! Didn't she realise she was haunting the wrong person? Maybe she was trying to use me. The ghost of the old Patty reaching out to the ghost of her younger self with me as go-between. Well, no way! No way! I stopped, as I reached the hall, and spun round. She was there all right. Grey and ghostly, but unmistakable.

"Just leave me alone!" I mouthed it, silently and furiously, up the stairs. "I don't want anything to do with you!"

CHAPTER FOURTEEN

A great tidal wave of excitement broke over me next morning. In just a few hours I would be with Alex! He was working until one o'clock, then going straight to Liverpool Street to catch the 1.30 train, arriving at Clacton an hour and a half later. I was going to meet him at the station. I wished so much that we could have spent the whole day together, but I knew I'd never be able to get away with it. It would be, *Where are you going, who are you going to meet?* They'd guess at once that it was Alex.

After breakfast, Maggie came round. She was staying up the road in a hotel and the Aunties had planned to take her out for the day. It was all working in my favour! They wouldn't get back till at least six o'clock. Alex and I could have the whole afternoon together. Yay! I was really hacked off when Auntie May took one look at the weather and announced, in her usual bossy fashion, that, "We shall wait until later. Let the rain clear."

Rather querulously, I said, "What does a bit of rain matter, if you're sitting in a car?"

"We do not intend," said Auntie May, "to spend the day just driving mindlessly about the countryside. A car is merely a means of transport from one place to another. In this case — " she turned graciously to Maggie — "we thought perhaps a visit to Flatford Mill?"

"I've heard of that," said Maggie.

"It was *painted*," said Ellie. "By some old artist guy."

"Constable, actually," I said. I wanted Maggie to know that one of us, at least, had a bit of culture.

Maggie said, "I love Constable! That would be great."

"Not in this weather." Auntie May was very firm about it. "We can just as easily go after lunch, so long as the rain gives over."

"It won't," said Ellie. "It never gives over. It's been doing it for days. I'm so *bored*!"

"She's always bored," I said.

"No inner resources," said Auntie May. "They're all dependent on technology, these days."

"Well, I'm not," said Maggie. "Who needs technology when they've got a brain?"

Auntie May sniffed. "Brain? They've forgotten how to use them!"

I resented that. I happen to use my brain quite a lot. When I'm researching on the computer, for instance, like for homework or something, I never just blindly copy what's there, I take the bits I need and

I put them into my own words. Also I read books. Also I *think*. Also I play computer games (though not as much as Ellie), but what's wrong with that? Just because Auntie May has never played them, and probably couldn't if she tried.

"Come on!" Maggie clapped her hands. "I challenge you. Pencil and paper! Can we find pencil and paper?"

Ellie, immediately suspicious, said, "What do we want pencil and paper for?"

"Games! What else?" Maggie laughed. "I told you, I come from a great family of games players!"

We play games, too, but mainly the sort where you're expected to get up and sing, or dance, or do some kind of comedy routine. The sort that Ellie loves and I just *hate*. The thought of pencil and paper quite cheered me up, though Ellie, naturally, was pulling faces.

"You don't have to look so scared," said Maggie. "They're only *games*!"

I said, "Brain games."

"Like taking exams," grumbled Ellie.

Hah! I always come top of exams. It would make a change from sweet little sis showing off and everyone applauding, while the boring old swotty pants just lumped about making an idiot of herself. I began to warm to Patty's granddaughter. Maybe *we* were the ones who were soul mates.

Auntie May came back with a supply of pens and writing pads and we all sat down at the kitchen table. Auntie Mo, rather nervously, wondered if perhaps she should just sit and watch. "I'm not very good at brain work."

"You never were," agreed Auntie May. "The only one of the family," she explained, "who had no academic ability. It probably would be best if she sat out."

"No, no, we can't have that!" said Maggie. "Nobody is allowed to sit out. I'll tell you what we'll do, we'll have teams. Me and Tamsin against the three of you. How about that?"

I was pleased – and flattered! – though I didn't think Auntie May was too happy with the arrangement. I'm not sure Ellie was, either, and poor Auntie Mo was plainly petrified. I felt quite sorry for her, but as Maggie reminded us, "We're just playing *games*. It's only a bit of fun!"

We sat there all morning, at the kitchen table, while the rain dripped and dropped outside and showed no signs of letting up. In spite of them *just being games*, some of us grew quite fiercely competitive. That is, me and Ellie, and Auntie May. We had games where you had to make lists, and games where you had to form words out of other words, and games where you had to quote poetry or book titles or the lyrics of songs. Every time Ellie's team scored a point Ellie went, "Yay!" and thumped on the table with her fist. Every time our team scored a point, or actually to be honest every time I scored one for us, I felt a rush of pride. I did so want Maggie to take notice and be impressed, so that when she went back to New Zealand and people asked her what we were like she would say, "Well, the younger one, Ellie, is very pretty and lively" (I *knew* she would say that; people always do) "but Tamsin, the older one, is *incredibly* bright." Oh, dear! Pathetic, I know; but we all have to have something we're proud of.

I was really glad that Maggie had chosen me as her partner. I would have hated to be with the Aunties! Auntie Mo was so flustered it was like her brain had shut down and she couldn't remember the simplest thing. At one point we were making lists of all the capital cities we could think of, and she wrote that "Stockport" was the capital of Sweden. Auntie May got so cross with her! She kept making these impatient tutting noises with her tongue, and rolling her eyes.

Maggie said, "OK, OK! Grand finale... limericks!"

Ellie said, "What's limericks?"

Auntie May tuttered. "Don't they teach you anything at school these days?"

I said, "Yes, they do! She did them last term, cos she got me to write one for her. *There was an old lady called Mary, whose chin was all horrid and hairy —* "

"I remember, I remember!" Ellie clapped her hands. Then she giggled and said, "It was rude!"

"We are not having rude ones," said Auntie May.

"Certainly not," agreed Maggie. "This is good clean family entertainment!" She said that we each had to write a first line and pass it to the person sitting next to us. "Just a bit of fun! We're not looking for masterpieces."

Auntie Mo pushed her chair back. "I do believe the rain is giving over," she said. "Maybe while you write your poems I should start preparing lunch?"

"Yes, you do that," said Auntie May, her pen already poised for action. "A good idea!"

Ellie was busy scribbling, her face all bunched up, her tongue clenched between her teeth. "Here!" She slid a sheet of paper towards me, looking at me slyly to see my reaction.

My face turned pink. I said, "What's this s'posed to be?"

In her sprawling hand she had written, *There was a boy who was called Alex.*

"I thought it would inspire you," said Ellie.

"Well, it doesn't! It's just stupid." I screwed up

the paper and hurled it across the room. "It's not even poetry!"

"Up to you to make it."

"Nobody could make it! The rhythm's all wrong."

"'Tisn't!"

"'Tis!"

"'Tisn't!

"T– "

"Be quiet! The pair of you." Auntie May threw down her pen. "If you can't be civilised, we had better call a halt. It's time, anyway. We don't want to leave it too late. Elinor, come with me, you can help get lunch. Tamsin, lay the table."

Auntie May swept out, Ellie trailing in her wake. At the door Ellie turned, and pulled a face. I gestured angrily.

Maggie seemed amused. "What was that about?"

I was almost tempted to pour out the whole story… how Mum and Dad were being so unfair, and so unreasonable: how I couldn't go on living if I wasn't allowed to see Alex. But after what she'd told us

★ 234 ☆

about Patty, and poor Frank, I wasn't too sure how she'd react. She might take the side of the grown-ups and agree with Mum and Dad that Alex was *too old* and *it wasn't appropriate*. So I just hunched a shoulder and said, "It's Ellie. She has absolutely no idea."

"Well, cheer up! It's not the end of the world." Maggie put an arm round my shoulder. "I reckon you and I did pretty well together… we make a good team! You'll have to come over on a visit some day. Maybe in your gap year. Do you have gap years?"

"Yes." I nodded, eagerly. "Before going to uni." And then I remembered: I wasn't going to uni. I was running away with Alex. "That is," I mumbled, "if I'm still here."

"What?" She laughed. "Why shouldn't you still be here?"

"I dunno." I flapped the tablecloth across the table. "Things happen."

Fortunately, before she could ask me what things, Ellie came bursting back in with a bunch of knives and forks. She tossed them down in a careless heap.

"You put those out properly," I said, "the way you're supposed to!"

"Laying the table's your job," said Ellie, flouncing off again.

Impatiently, I snatched them up and began to set them out, the way the Aunties liked. "We don't do this at home," I said. "It's only when we're staying with the Aunties."

"Yeah, well, I expect they have their little ways," said Maggie. "People do, when they get old."

I was about to ask her, "Did Patty have her little ways?" when Ellie came clattering through the door again, carrying plates. I gave up. It obviously wasn't the right time for a conversation.

The rain had finally slowed to a drizzle, so after lunch Auntie May went to get the car out. Maggie seemed surprised, and even disappointed, that I wasn't going with them. I told her what I had told the Aunties, that I had to visit the library to do some research for a school project.

"On a Saturday?" she said.

"Well, I had to, like… book time on the computer?" I did wish I could have told Maggie the truth. I don't *enjoy* telling lies; it's just that sometimes they give you no choice. Well, the aunties gave me no choice. Maggie would have been more sympathetic. She would have been on my side!

"It seems such a shame," she said. "You're going to miss out on all the fun."

I said, "I know, and I'm really sorry… but I have been to Flatford lots of times before."

"So have I," said Ellie. "Maybe I should go to the library too."

I looked at her sharply. Could she possibly suspect? It was a nasty moment, saved, fortunately, by Maggie. "Oh, now, you can't both desert me!" she said. "One of you must keep me company… Ellie, you could tell me all about your acting. I want to know!"

Ellie brightened; she liked that idea. I immediately felt wildly jealous. For a moment I almost wished that I was the one that was going and she was the one staying behind. If I had been going I could have told Maggie all that I knew about Constable. Ellie knew next to nothing, but I had read all about him in the booklet we'd got last time we'd visited. I knew loads!

I tried to give her a few facts as they were on the way out to the car, but Auntie May said briskly that we didn't have time for that. "We need to be going."

"You could always change your mind and come with us," said Maggie. "You know what they say... all work and no play?"

For a moment I was actually tempted. But then I reminded myself that I was going to meet Alex. *I was going to meet Alex!* How could I even have thought of going with them?

Suddenly I couldn't wait for them all to be off. The minute the front door closed I turned and rushed upstairs - only to come to an abrupt halt at the top. There on the landing was a familiar grey shape, faint and floating, shrouded in mist. *Patty.* For the first time,

I felt a twinge of apprehension. I am not scared of ghosts… but I was in the house on my own! There were the old ladies, living in their rooms on the other side of the partition, but what use would they be? They couldn't come to my rescue! And then I thought, well, but what harm could *she* do? She was an old lady herself. What was more, she was a *dead* old lady. And she was trying to ruin my big day! The day I'd been looking forward to for so long. How would she have liked it if some stupid old interfering busybody of a ghost had hung around when she was going off to meet Frank?

"I wish you would just *give up*," I said. "I'm sorry things didn't work out, but that is no reason to come here haunting *me*."

And with that I brushed crossly past. I didn't have time to waste communing with ghosts! I had barely half an hour to wash my hair and change my clothes.

When I came out of the bathroom, my hair wrapped in a towel, the landing was empty. Just a faint hint of reproach seemed to hang in the air, like, "How could you do this to me?"

I don't know why it made me feel guilty. *I* hadn't asked to be haunted.

CHAPTER FIFTEEN

I was almost late. I couldn't believe it! I'd waited *so long* to be with Alex, and now I was having to tear up the road with my heart hammering, praying that I got there before the train. I just made it! As I pelted into the station, I saw him coming through the barrier. I waved and called out.

"Alex! Over here!"

He turned, and saw me, and his face lit up. He walked towards me, smiling, and oh, I'd forgotten how beautiful he was! The next minute I was flying into his arms and we were pressed together, kissing like we were never going to stop. Like the world had come to a standstill and we were locked in each other's embrace for eternity. I was dimly aware, in some distant part of my brain, that there were people all about us. That some of these people might just know the Aunties, they might even know *me*. But what did I care? Alex and I were back together and nothing and no one could separate us!

I don't know how long we stood there, enclosed in our little private bubble of time. Maybe minutes, maybe only seconds. But it felt like for ever. Finally, reluctantly, we broke apart. Alex took my hand and we moved slowly towards the exit. To my dismay I saw that the rain had started coming down again. Quite heavily too.

"Where we go?" said Alex.

"I don't know!" The words came wailing out of me. I'd imagined us sitting on the beach, golden and glowing, soaking up the sunshine. Now what were we going to do? I didn't dare go back to the Aunties'. I supposed we could always find a café somewhere and sit down, but then there would be other people. I didn't want other people! I wanted to be on my own, with Alex.

"Maybe if we went down to the sea front," I said, "we could huddle in one of the shelters."

"OK! We do that. We go!"

Alex took my hand and we made a mad dash out of the station. The rain was sploshing all about us, bouncing off the rooftops and splatting in the gutter. After a few seconds Alex stopped and took off his jacket. He said, "Here! You wear." I tried to protest, but he was insistent. He said it didn't matter if he got wet, he didn't mind a bit of rain.

"I dry later. No problem!"

I thought that I could also dry later, and why should he be the one to get wet, just because he was a man? But I also thought that it was nice to be spoilt for once, even though it was not very feminist. Katie would have had a right go at me, she is really into feminism. So am I, as a rule. But Alex was so sweet and old-fashioned! He was what Auntie May would call a *gentleman*. I felt a bit guilty, but I didn't give him his jacket back. Instead, I snuggled inside it as we pounded along the sea front in search of a shelter that wasn't already occupied.

We found one at last and instantly fell into each other's arms, soaking though Alex was, and me with my hair all dripping. But being wet didn't seem to matter. Being together was all that mattered.

Vaguely I became aware of another couple about to cram into the shelter with us, but they obviously thought better of it and moved on. They could see we didn't want company!

"Tamsin, I miss you so much," said Alex. "You miss me?"

"Like crazy," I said. "So much that it hurts! I've been counting the days. I've been counting the minutes! But you'll never believe –"

Pause, while we kiss. *"You'll never believe – "*

Another pause. *"You'll never believe the things that have been happening!"*

I was so full of news. Bursting with news! I wanted to tell him Patty's story. How she and Frank had run off together. How she'd been haunting me. I wanted to tell him about Maggie. How she'd come all the way from New Zealand specially to meet the family.

"They've all gone off for the day, but I daren't take you back in case anyone sees. If Auntie May found out, we'd be in huge big trouble."

"We be all right here," said Alex. He laughed. "Like our own little place!"

"But it's horrible," I said, "having to creep round like we're a couple of criminals!"

"Soon all be over." Alex pulled me to him. "We be together all the time. You, me… no trouble! No one say he too old, you too young… you be sixteen. All OK!"

Why did a little cold shiver run down my spine when he said that? Why, suddenly, did I find myself shrinking back?

You'll have to come over on a visit someday. Maybe in your gap year...

I wasn't going to have a gap year. Katie would have one! She'd go on to uni, just like we'd planned. She'd still be there, at school, working away without me. People would wonder where I was. Katie would tell them, "She's run off with her boyfriend." Yesterday, it had seemed so romantic! Just *yesterday*. I'd been so sure it was what I wanted. So certain that I couldn't live without Alex. Why was I starting to have doubts? What was happening to me?

Alex smiled, reassuringly. "No more worry, Tamsin. No problem."

He didn't know. *He didn't know.*

I said, "Alex ..."

"No talk!" He laid a finger on my lips. "Too much talk!"

"But A – "

"Tsh!"

"But – "

"I say, no talk!"

It would have been so easy to give in. Just to let things happen. I loved him so desperately! Surely that should be enough?

But I knew that it wasn't. I knew that I had to tell him. I had to break it to him. I said, "Alex – " And then I burst into tears and the truth finally came blurting out.

"Alex, I lied! I'm only thirteen … I won't be sixteen for another two years!"

I realise now – now that I really *am* almost sixteen – that I did a very terrible thing, deceiving Alex. I could have got him into so much trouble! And he could have been so angry with me. I know how fortunate I am that he was such a sweet and gentle person. Lots of boys would have been furious. Most people would probably say they had a right to be. But Alex wasn't like that – which actually, in some ways, made things worse. If he'd yelled at me, I would at least have felt that I was getting what I deserved. That I was being properly *punished*. Instead, he just went very quiet. He seemed, like… dazed. As if he couldn't quite get his head round it. And it didn't matter how many times I said that *I was sorry, I was so sorry*, I knew that I had hurt him.

I remembered him telling me how Marta hadn't believed I was as old as I said I was. How Alex had laughed and said, "She just jealous!" Did he remember that? I should have told him then, all that time ago. I shouldn't have let him go on believing a lie.

Yet what did it matter? Fourteen, fifteen? What difference did it make? We still loved each other!

I tried to say this to him. I tried to believe it… age wasn't important! But maybe it is, when you're only thirteen. In my heart of hearts, I think I knew it. Alex knew it, too.

"Tamsin," he said, "this cannot be!"

I wept, and I pleaded, but he shook his head. "I love you, Tamsin. I love you so much! But this is not right."

I sobbed and protested that love was always right. Alex said, "I wish this is true. But is not. And you cannot be here with me like this. I understand, now, why your mum, she get mad. Is my fault!" He tapped his chest. "Even though I believe you nearly sixteen, I know you not *yet* sixteen. So I the one doing the wrong."

It nearly cracked me up when he said that. How could he possibly blame himself?

"I think you must go now, Tamsin. Please! You go."

"I can't!" I wept. "I can't leave you!"

"Tamsin." He held me away from him, looking at me quite sternly. "You only thirteen. I too old! Your mum, she know this. You also, you know this. This why you say to me you nearly sixteen."

"I didn't want you to think I was just a stupid little baby!"

"I never think you stupid little baby. I love you! I always love you. For me, you the best thing that ever happened. I so lonely before I meet you! You bring me much joy. Much happiness. But now is time to say goodbye."

He let me walk back with him to the station, but he wouldn't let me wait to see him off. He gave me one final kiss, very innocently on my forehead, and that was it. The last time I saw him. We spoke just once more on the phone; the saddest conversation I have ever had. I wept and pleaded, but Alex was firm. He said, "I love you, Tamsin. But is not right."

I cried into my pillow, quietly and fiercely, trying to keep it from Ellie, for three nights in a row; until gradually, almost without my noticing, little by little, I started to feel less miserable. I found myself one day, shortly before Mum came back from tour, confiding in Maggie. She was due to fly home to New Zealand the following week, and I felt I had to talk to her. She listened in sympathetic silence as I poured it all out, and then she said, "It sounds to me as if your Alex is a very lovely young man," which just set me off crying all over again.

"It also sounds to me," said Maggie, "as if he's a very honourable young man. He did do the right thing, you know."

I nodded, through my tears. I knew that he had. I said, "I think your gran was trying to warn me."

"My gran?" Maggie sounded surprised. "What makes you say that?"

So then I told her about the ghostly form on the upstairs landing, and how I'd recognised it as Patty. "I don't know whether she was trying to get through to *me*, or to herself when she was young."

"She was certainly trying to get through to someone," said Maggie. "Those were almost her last words… *I can't get through to her.*"

We had a long talk all about Patty and Frank – and ghosts – and how easy it was to get carried away by love. Maggie said we must be sure to keep in touch, and we have; we email all the time. Mum has said if I like, before starting at uni, I can fly out to New Zealand to stay with Maggie and her partner, Jeff. I'm really looking forward to that!

Katie and I made up. She didn't gloat or say *I told you so* when I admitted that Alex and I had broken up. She is a true friend. I can see now how difficult it must have been for her, with me having a boyfriend and her being left on her own. She must have felt deserted. Maybe even a bit jealous. I know this because last term it was Katie who had a boyfriend and me who was on my own and *I hated it*. It made me desperate for Alex all over again. Fortunately it didn't go on too long as I started seeing this boy from Year 11, Dillon Mackenzie. We're sort of an item, though it isn't anything serious. I mean, we're not in love, or anything. I told Maggie that I didn't think I would ever love anyone the way I'd loved Alex, and she agreed that I probably wouldn't. She said that your first love is very special.

"But you will love again. I promise! It won't be the same, but in its own way it will be just as exciting."

I find that really hard to imagine. On the other hand I do think Maggie is quite a wise person and knows what she's talking about. As long as I live, I'll remember the few wonderful months that I had with Alex. I'll remember the way he smiled, the way his eyes used to crinkle up. I'll remember the touch of his hand, warm and a little bit rough, and the feel of his arm round me. I really did love him, so very, very much. But maybe, one day…

I caught a glimpse of Alex the other week, just fleetingly, from the top of a bus. My heart immediately started churning, and I felt this mad impulse to jump off at the next stop and go running back; and then I saw that he was with a girl, and that they were holding hands, and for a moment I felt devastated. But then after a bit the feeling passed, and a sort of peace came over me. I craned my neck, looking back out of the bus window, and I discovered that I didn't feel upset at the thought of some other girl holding his hand. Instead I felt glad for him. I want so much for him to be happy!

I told Maggie that same evening, in an email. *I thought it would hurt but it really didn't. I just felt glad, for his sake. But I do still love him! I don't understand what this means. How can you love someone and be happy that they're with someone else?*

Maggie emailed straight back: *It's precisely because you*

love Alex that you can be happy for him. Now you must move on and be happy for yourself.

Well, I am! There are so many things waiting to happen. Year 12 next year – Katie and I think we might go to sixth-form college. That will be fun! Then there will be my gap year in New Zealand, then uni. And maybe *one* day I will meet someone else and fall in love. I'm beginning to feel a bit more hopeful.

But it doesn't mean that I will ever forget Alex.

Buy more great books by

Jean Ure

direct from HarperCollins with FREE postage and packing in the UK.

Fortune Cookie	978-0-00-722462-3
Star Crazy Me	978-0-00-722461-6
Hunky Dory	978-0-00-722460-9
Gone Missing	978-0-00-722459-3
The Moon	978-0-00-716464-6
Boys Beware	978-0-00-716138-6
Sugar and Spice	978-0-00-716137-9